Other Books by
Bill Rebane

"Film Funding 2000"

From Roswell

With Love

Bill Rebane

Exploration Press
Saxon, WI

To my wife, Barbara, the super woman
without whom little would get done
My four children, twelve grandchildren
and three great grandchildren, a diverse
mix of personalities and temperaments.

Prologue

The future of man kind hangs in the balance. To avoid the near inevitable may lie in the past.

A half century of cover ups by the government and the secrets of a handful of people belonging to a very secret society, will clash.

The incident at the site near Roswell was largely ignored by the scientific and industrial community, until recently, where it not for another mystery two thousand miles away, a mystery as bizarre and significant as the crash near Roswell itself.

Something has triggered the wheels into motion of every intelligent agency on the planet, attempting to get to the bottom of the real secrets of Roswell.

Suddenly over fifty years later, the joke could well be on those who perpetrated the cover up and in the process missed the purpose, if not the reasons for the entire earth shaking event, foretold in the lost book of Nostradamus.

Saving humanity and life on earth may depend greatly on how society reacts to the demands of those that have the answers, to the needs of all the people on this planet, Earth.

Chapter 1

1947

Rockland, nestled in the rugged wilderness of the Upper Peninsula of Michigan, population approximately 150, is bathed in the soft glow of moonlight the night of July 2, 1947. A car traveling on the highway through this wooded, hilly area comes to a sudden, screeching, sliding halt on Highway 45 just south of Rockland.

The driver side door of the Chev Impala is thrust open to allow the six-foot, 260 pound frame of Reick Hautala to emerge from his vehicle and stand silently, awestruck, beside it, gazing at a now innocent night sky. His exit from the car was instantaneous and impulsive. He was compelled by what he had just seen, though what he had witnessed would be overshadowed by events occurring over two thousand miles to the southwest only moments later that would boggle the global scientific community, and billions around the earth as well, for decades to come.

Reick has observed objects, strange objects in the night skies over the UP before but nothing like what he has seen tonight. Out of the corner of his eye he had caught a flash of bright light in the upper, far visual reaches of the northeastern firmament. It was similar to what he had seen many times before over Lake Superior on his 36 foot Chris

Craft while fishing for trout and lake salmon, or on long drives home from the lake late at night.

This time it was different. He had seen a lot more than the usual bright light that flashed and disappeared into oblivion as fast as one could blink an eye. What Reick had observed was a phenomena. The flash that got his attention turned into a gray outline of an object, a disc-shaped object, glowing intermittently. Then, a split second later, something incomprehensible happened. Something strange was happening up there to the object.

Something had parted from the saucer-shaped thing and, like a fiery meteor, had descended vertically toward the earth. The disc-shaped object seemed to quiver before changing its trajectory and continued its light-speed decent into the southwestern sky. It reminded Reick of bird hunting when he had just winged the bird. It would glide on until the wings gave out and it would plummet to the ground. Reick scanned the full horizon one more time before uttering a few words in his native Finnish, pressing his body back behind the Chevy's steering wheel.

A half-hour later Reick was sitting in a small tavern in Bruce Crossing, Michigan, sharing this evening sighting with the establishment's patrons. Normally skeptical, they had heard Reick's stories before. But something was different this night. This time they listened intently. Just a half-hour before Reick's arrival a flash of bright light had drawn every customer in the bar to rush outside where they were baffled by tremors from the earth beneath their feet.

There are no earthquakes in this part of the country, yet residents within a 20 mile radius of the Little Finlandia Tavern reported similar vibrations.

That very same night, at precisely the same time as the earth trembled, a strange light appeared on the ground, deep in the national forest near Paulding, Michigan, only   a stone's throw away from Bruce Crossing, Rockland and just North of Watersmeet.

Chapter 2

Bayfield, Wisconsin, the most northern geographical point in the State of Wisconsin, serving as the gateway to the Apostle Islands, is an ideal location for amateur astronomer Jason Roberts, a self-described scientist 'extraordinaire,' to observe the heavens.

He loved Bayfield because it resembled the New England fishing village where he grew up. Instead of the Atlantic Ocean, the great Lake Superior provided the ambiance he was accustomed to in his boyhood. His small, but impressive, house stands high on a hill where he could not only see the entire Village of Bayfield and its quaint harbor, but most of the legendary Apostle Island chain. His two-story Victorian house's location has served his stargazing activities well. Where once a widow-walk had circled the house's steeple-style turret, it had been replaced with an aluminum dome sheltering an observatory with a sophisticated telescope housed inside.

Whatever Jason Roberts does for the Society is no more than what others with similar enthusiasm and talents did for the organization's cause. This time around though, he was doing something very special. Maybe for the world as a whole, but the Society would understand its value more than anyone else, because whatever Reick Hautala had seen the night of July 2, 1947, Jason had captured on 35-mm film through the high powered telescope in his small, but sophisticated, observatory.

But no one, and he meant no one, except the Star Light Society would learn from him what had happened this night and how. His fingers trembled as he unloaded the Bell and Howell Eymo 35-mm camera with an attached periscope viewfinder.

He had seen the object and had to act fast. He had kept his eyes on the telescope eyepiece, set the film speed on the camera from still motion to 24-frames per second hoping to capture it all.

While 35-mm movie film is an expensive proposition, this time, with a split-second decision, he opted to run the camera at normal speed, praying that the 100-foot roll of film, maximum for this camera, would not run out before he had captured the full event.

This would be the first time in the history of UFOlogy that an unidentified flying object had been caught on film with problems, if not a major system failure. Something very bizarre had happened up there while the camera purred away. All he could do is hope that whatever he had observed was captured clearly and accurately on that 100 foot spool of film.

As a whole, he could depend on his Bell and Howell Eymo, one of the most rugged film cameras ever made. This rugged piece of equipment had served him well throughout his years as a war correspondent and Army Corps of Engineers cameraman.

The camera had been through one hell of a lot of action during World War II, from Anzio to Normandy, to the Battle of the Bulge. It had been lost in the mud of battles, been submerged in water, and even dropped from a plane at 10,000 feet. Yet, it had survived and had delivered the goods on film that ended up on American theater screens as newsreel footage from World War II.

The thought that it could fail him now was absurd. Nevertheless, images of his experiences with his precious camera flashed through his mind as he unscrewed the camera from the mount on the telescope. The entire event had taken no more than 20 seconds.

At this very moment, while unloading the film in his darkroom he used the extra precaution of a camera changing bag. He didn't even trust his red darkroom light. Jason knew that he had captured it all just as he had seen it. The film would stand as indisputable evidence that flying saucers did exist.

What Jason did not know at this point in time is what was going on in the desert near Roswell, New Mexico, an event that would turn the U.S. government upside down, shake up the world's scientific community, baffle the public and create a new purpose and a new secret movement called the Starlight Society. What Jason Roberts had on film would, more than a half-century later, shake up the United States Government, and a few other governments as well.

Chapter 3

Roswell New Mexico July 2nd, 1947

Army surgical nurse Rachel Dunham was
rudely awakened at an ungodly hour and ordered to
report to the hospital immediately. *What the hell happened?* she thought to herself. She couldn't figure it
out. World War II was over. The boys were home and
there had not been any life-threatening emergencies
requiring her skills since she returned from Frankfurt,
Germany over a year ago.

Before that, she had spent two years in the
European theater of war. As a front-line battle nurse,
she had experienced it all right up to the time the allies
had divided up the Reich upon the fall of Berlin.

By this time in her life she had seen more
blood and guts and had stitched up more flesh than
any other person on the base at Fort Douglas, New
Mexico.

*"What the hell had happened now? What was the
big rush? Above all, why me?"* she wondered to herself
as she threw on her clothes. Without a cup of coffee
or any hot nourishment, she rushed out to the waiting jeep that was to deliver her to the hospital and to
something that would first horrify her and then forever change her life.

Chapter 4

The Pentagon

Just an hour earlier Colonel Blanchard also experienced something he would have never expected to see happen in his military career. He had just entered his office, a cup of coffee in hand, when the telephone rang. He slid into the wooden office chair with armrests while picking up the receiver on the third double ring. He did not have a chance to sit very long. After the voice on the other end of the line identified himself, Col. Blanchard jumped out of his chair and stood at attention.

"Yes, Mr. President," he said, "Colonel Blanchard here." Realizing that he was alone in his office, and there was no need to stand at attention, he slowly redeposited himself back into his chair. Only after listening to the caller's inquiry did he answer, "Yes, Mr. President, we have four bodies: three dead, one alive." There was a pause allowing Blanchard to collect himself from this unexpected call. The conversation ended with; "Yes sir, Mr. President, be assured."

Chapter 5

The Army Military Police corporal escorted nurse Rachel Dunham into the conference room of the hospital where she faced a half-a-dozen officers for what was explained to her as an essential briefing on a top secret subject.

Major Baker from a Pentagon information office was the first to speak, turning directly to Lt. Nurse Dunham in a solemn voice, "Lt. Dunham, you are being ordered to not only provide your professional skills but, your skills of maintaining the highest degree of secrecy of the mission you are about to participate in."

Lt. Rachel Dunham could do nothing but acquiesce to what were not requests but just plain old orders.

Chapter 6

In a dark narrow hallway in the far wing and the lower levels of the hospital two soldiers wearing helmet liners are carrying a stretcher covered with a white sheet. They are rushing. As they round the corner of the narrow hall, an arm belonging to the body on the stretcher dangles out from under the sheet covering it.

Only at closer observation would one notice that the arm, the hand and fingers in particular, resemble a spindly, long emaciated woman. In rounding the narrow corner, the front stretcher bearer is forced against the gray brick wall dislodging his helmet liner which tumbles to the floor. In the process of retrieving his helmet liner, Private Jerry Bates notices the dangling arm. His gloved hand reaches for it and quickly places it under the sheet on the stretcher. Only one more hallway to go before they've completed their mission.

Private Jerry Bates is sick to his stomach. The odor from what is ever under the blanket is about to make him throw up. Good God, what was happening here, he thought. Private Bates would never know. He died one month later from very unnatural causes.

Chapter 7

The cover-up had begun. The United States government would continue to treat the events at Roswell that fateful night of July 2, 1947, as top secret, covered up by the weather balloon story that emerged as a planned public relations campaign created by the Pentagon press corps.

In the same time it took for the government to devise and spread the weather balloon story through newspapers and radio in America, Jason Roberts was able to develop his 35-mm film.

The results were sensational, something the Star Light Society would embrace, and protect for over half-a-century. They would energize the Society, give it a renewed purpose, and swell its membership ranks to huge international proportions.

While the Star Light Society grew to a membership of hundreds of thousands around the world, only a handful of Society executives knew the secrets of the film footage and the details of the ongoing events at Roswell.

Speculation continued despite government attempts to convince the general public otherwise. Too many witnesses said otherwise.

The government spin doctors were convinced they had iced the story. But unbeknownst to them, the Star Light Society members were working cleverly and secretly under cover to unspin the Roswell incident. Some were working their way into inner circles of even the U.S. Army's military police, medical staffs and other government agencies involved in the initial cover-up of the Roswell UFO crash.

Chapter 8

60 years later

It is a massive, beautiful old library built around 1889 and the City of Milwaukee is proud of it. Arturo Smith, dressed in a long winter coat, swiftly moves up the wide and antiquated stairs to the second floor reading room. Only a few isolated patrons are studying there, not noticing Smith's arrival in the reading section of this huge room, where a person could easily get lost between the many shelves bearing the knowledge and writings of thousands of authors.

Smith casually disappears between one of the aisles but quickly emerges with several books that he places on one of the huge beautiful antique library tables where he casually settles down and pretends to become deeply involved in the writings. If he is not completely immersed in the subject matter in front of him, it certainly looks as though he is. He remains on guard. Only a trained observer would notice that in reality Smith is not interested in the books at all, but rather throwing anticipatory glances toward the entrance of the reading room as if expecting someone. A casual observer might sense that he was trying to avoid detection. But, no.

He is joined by a gentlemen dressed in a black winter overcoat with matching black hat who, with out invitation, takes a seat opposite Smith at the huge table.

"You Mr. Smith ?" the man in the black coat asks.

Smith nods and acknowledges, "Yes, I am."

The man in black identifies himself as simply, "I'm Sheldon," and with no more words, reaches into his coat pocket producing a packet of postcard size documents inside a protective plastic zippered pouch. As Sheldon slides the documents toward Smith, he intones, "Your papers, everything you need is in there. Study the information and commit it to memory. You understand our concerns."

Smith nods and adds, "Of course."

But Sheldon is not done, "and remember the clothing. Dress as others do, you know, not to stand out or look different. And, good luck."

Smith looks up at Sheldon, nods with under-standing and repeats, "Good luck."

"Sure." Sheldon rises, pivots and simply walks out without further ado. Arturo Smith is alone again, at least within himself.

Chapter 9

Roughly 450 miles north.

Visibility for the driver of the late model, dark green Ford Explorer is down to nearly zero. A blizzard rages, called a lake-effect storm with a fierce nor'easter driving the huge white flakes horizontally across the road, obliterating the view for Arturo Smith, the driver. The blinding snow is making it impossible to see, let alone read any road signs, that were provided him as part of directions to the Whispering Pines Lodge.

The far upper reaches of northern Wisconsin and Michigan's Upper Peninsula hugging the Lake Superior's shores are prone to sudden, severe weather and extreme winter conditions with snow accumulation of eight to nine feet annually.

But Mr. Smith is a determined driver, steadfast behind the wheel of the four-by-four SUV which has a tough time making it on the as yet unplowed road.

Chapter 10

The lodge was built in the early 1930s. In its heydays it had served as the northern hideaway and playground for vacationers from as far away as Milwaukee and Chicago.

Located in the middle of pristine wilderness areas, near the Wisconsin/Michigan border, it was barely accessible during the early part of the 20th century.

The clientele in those days would travel by train to Hurley, Wisconsin or Ironwood, Michigan, then continue by either horse-drawn carriage or automobile east toward Watersmeet, Michigan. The unpaved roads leading north from Milwaukee and Chicago or Madison, Wisconsin, for that matter, in those days were a real challenge for those traveling by car. There were long stretches with no services and roads that challenged the springs and shocks of the best built automobiles. Nevertheless, the tourists and vacationers came in large numbers, attracted by the beauty of this pristine northern wilderness, hundreds of virgin lakes for the fishing enthusiasts, an abundance of wildlife for hunters in the fall and plenty of snow for skiers and those who enjoyed the legendary sleigh rides the lodge offered during the Christmas and New Year seasons.

The lodge was rustic, opulent and built for

the ultimate in comfort, offering its guests the best
of food, guides, and a variety of other services and
essential amenities   necessary for a discriminating
clientele.   Today the lodge is little more then a
shadow of that era. It has seen better days. Eleanor
Madsen, the lady of the house, had inherited the estate
from her grandfather some 25 years ago. There was a
big estate with much land, but little cash to maintain
it. Antiquated old lodges were going out of style in
the late 20th century and were being replaced by more
contemporary resort offerings. No indoor pool, no hot
tub and sauna's, no business. Even though Eleanor
sold off 40-acre parcel after 40-acre parcel to keep up
with rising property taxes and the maintenance of an
old wood structure that always needed fixing, especially after a harsh winter.

The old lodge was downsized into a bed and
breakfast for discriminating guests who yearned for
the atmosphere and living style of the good old days,
a beautiful wilderness setting and peace and quiet.

At the same time, the old lodge was home and
provided for a good and gracious living for Eleanor
and her daughter Gail. Business was fairly brisk in
the summer time when the fishing season opened and
stayed busy through the summer when the recreation-
al activities of the many lakes beckoned the tourists
north.

Chapter 11

The single amber light illuminating the ornate sign of the Bed and Breakfast Lodge over the entrance-way indicated to Smith that he has reached his destination. He had to make several local stops in the village of Light Struck, Michigan to inquire about the establishment where arrangements had been made for him to stay for several weeks.

The one and only service station in the town gave him precise directions and suggested that he wait till morning after the plows came through. But he needed to get there as quickly as possible, so he carefully followed the directions given him realizing full well the challenge that was to come if the vehicle could not make it through the 15-inch accumulation of snow cover. The fact that this snowfall consisted of mostly powder, the light and fluffy stuff, helped Smith to get there without any mishaps. The sign under the light assured him he was at the right place.

Smith takes the aluminum suit case from the passenger side seat and proceeds to exit from the vehicle.

The door is opened by Eleanor Madsen before Smith reaches the set of steps leading up to the entrance.

"You must be Mr. Smith?" she asked, extending her hand to the late evening guest. Smith nods, temporarily placing the suitcase next to him on the porch and takes her extend hand in greeting. "Come on in and get out of the snow. Wasn't at all sure if you would make it tonight with this weather and all, and the plow won't be here until tomorrow morning. Come on, come on in."

Once inside, Eleanor just keeps on talking. Guests and conversing with them was one of her favorite pastimes. "I bet you could use a good hot cup of coffee, or tea, or a cup of hot chocolate, maybe?" she asks.

"Coffee, yes, thank you. Caffeine always helps me to relax." As Smith follows her to an area of the lodge that is used to serve the meals to the Bed & Breakfast guests. It is too small to have been the main dining room of the old lodge or the great room. The latter is now simply not in use and remains unheated during the winter season.

The small sitting and dining room adjacent to the kitchen is overcrowded with antiquities of all sorts Rosenthal and Meissen porcelain, a crystal and ornate silverware collection intermixed with more contemporary pieces of art and curios in form of sculptures and paintings. Glass china cabinets cover the walls leaving almost too little space for the massive oak table which can be extended to seat six-to-eight people, depending on the season and the number of guests at any given time. Any space not taken up by Eleanor's collectible treasures are filled with plants. To be sure, there are no empty areas on the shelves and in the glass display cabinets. The setting is complimented by the illumination emanating from three 19th century Tiffany lamps with bead fringes and one unique crystal chandelier almost too overpowering, considering the room size.

"Please, have a seat. There is a coat rack right behind you near the hall. I'll be right back with our coffee."

Smith relieves himself of the bulky overcoat and the aluminum suitcase and seats himself at the oak table with four chairs surrounding it.

Just minutes later, Eleanor enters with a silver serving tray holding the coffee and all the condiment and serving essentials.

"We don't usually have guests at this time of the year. What brings you to this Godforsaken place in the middle of winter?" she asks as she proceeds to pour the coffee.

"Peace and quiet. I'm a writer."

Eleanor is all ears. "Really? A writer? What a coincidence. My daughter is a writer." She reaches for the sugar and cream, gesturing to Smith.

He shakes his head and simply says, "Black, thank you. What does your daughter write? What genre?"

"News. Gail is a reporter for the local newspaper but will she be happy to meet you, a fellow writer. What kind of stuff do you write Mr. Smith?" She doesn't give him a chance to answer. She rambles on, in her element. "Murder mysteries ... science fiction?"

His face is filled with the suggestion of a 'yes' answer, if he could only squeeze it in, but he listens patiently and smiles gently as she continues.

"Well, you've come to the right place. You'll

get a lot of peace and quiet here. I'll guarantee it. Sleepy town, this is. All winter long. Nothing ever happens around here except for the snowmobilers that come to see the mystery light, one of our local tourist attractions."

"Interesting," Smith replies. "You must tell me more about it sometime."

"I'd love to, and surely we can make arrangements for you to see it yourself, if they plow the roads that is."

"Just how far is this mystery light?"

"A couple of miles, or as we say around here, just down the road a piece."

Pretending he fully understands. "I see, Ms. Madsen."

"Just call me Eleanor, and you're Mr. A. Smith. What's the 'A' stand for?"

"Arturo, and please call me Arturo."

She repeats it pronouncing it carefully. "A-r-t-u-r-o. What an interesting name. Where does it come from? I mean what nationality?"

Smith seems puzzled for a second, then catches himself. "It's universal ... Yes, I think that would be the correct description. It's universal."

Now, Eleanor seems confused. While she has not traveled widely, she is an intelligent woman. Her lack of travel to other countries has been compensated by being an avid reader and a fanatical television viewer. "Arturo," she repeats again. "Most interesting first name. I like it."

Smith looks at her with interest and nods.

She takes his gesture as a sign of being tired and, realizing that it is getting late, says, "You must be tired, and I've not even shown you to your room yet. It's upstairs. Would you like to get settled in?" She continues as they stand. "Any more luggage?"

There is no answer as Smith takes the coat from the rack and reaches for his aluminum suitcase.

"Of course, if you don't need it, whatever it is, you can always get it in the morning when it stops snowing." She adds, as they reach the base of the stair-well, "of course, there is no guarantee of that, I mean for it to stop snowing." Her voice begins to trail as they ascend to the upper floor.

Chapter 12

Washington , D.C., The Pentagon

    Evan Kirkland is furious as he throws a bundled stack of papers on the conference table near his desk. "Why now? And why, of all places, the Upper Peninsula of Michigan?" .

    Amber Winslow, a sexy looking blonde in her early thirties, is comfortably leaning into the high-backed arm chair positioned in the corner opposite Evan's desk. Her legs cross, making the lower part of her dress appear like a mini skirt. She has a smirk on her face as she answers Evan. "How in the hell would I know? All I know is the information comes right from the top."

    Ignoring the answer, he seats himself. "I'm well familiar with that part of the country. Yooper land -- nothing but Godforsaken wilderness and few people. Good for nature-loving tourists in the summer." Evan stands again, taking the wide rubber band off the bundle of documents and sorts out the file folders carefully laying them out on the conference table.

    Evan Kirkland is a man in his fifties looking more like a disheveled university professor then a Pentagon employee. In his early days in Washington he was attached to an Air Force research team working on "Project Blue Book." He was a handy man for the government to have around, holding degrees in science, aeronautics, chemistry and journalism. Anything that baffled the secret Washington establishment, their answer is Evan Kirkland, the avid researcher with superb analytical skills.

Physically, Evan does not fit the Defense Department mold. He could be a good looking man under the long white hair, the beard and the unpressed attire, but Evan does not care. He hates bureaucrats, the secrecy game and most of all the pressures the agencies put on him when they needed his help to solve a problem. In all, Evan is his own man who attempts to maintain a sense of humor among all that seriousness and secrecy that goes on around him.

Amber is watching him carefully as he attempts to organize his papers. She secretly admires him and is jealous of the respect he commands from his coworkers and those positioned in the capital's highest places. Amber is educated and intelligent but upset that, at age thirty-three, she is not being appreciated or recognized for her talents, which she believes lie in the area of the Secret Service, the FBI or even the CIA. Not even her hourglass figure has helped her to get her vivacious curves into the spy game, a game she loves.

She did have four good years in the White House as a White House aide occasionally working with the oval office. Clinton loved her curves and her long blond hair but not her independent attitude. She looked right through him and knew every time she was near him what he wanted -- the same thing he got from others, but not from her. Being the detective she was and always wanted to be, of course, she knew all about Monica if not the whole scenario in detail.

She also knew how things worked in Washington and who does whom and what goes on behind closed doors. She wonders if she had been a little more promiscuous, she could have attained her goals, getting bumped into the CIA, or pumped by a whole set of hypocritical bastards that make the decisions. She may be a blonde with all the right curves but she is also a conservative old-fashioned girl from Oshkosh, Wisconsin with virtues and values that in today's Washington have become a career detriment to advancement -- unless she was willing to cash in on the assets. She is not just going to allow herself to be screwed to the top.

As she watches Evan fumble through the papers on the conference table, she wonders about this assignment. It's top secret and will be filled with intrigue. It's not spy work but what the hell, it's interesting. Besides, she took a liking to Evan. He seemed like a fun guy, super intelligent and a straight character.

"Wasn't the Upper Peninsula of Michigan the hot bed for the militia movement in the early and mid-nineties?" she asks.

Evan looks at her. *Damn, she is pleasant to look at, he thinks to himself.* "You're right, according to the old FBI files, but that has nothing to do with this."

"Maybe nothing, maybe a lot," Amber counters.

"OK, let's have it. What do you mean?"

Amber stands. The hem of her dress falling below the knees now, revealing less of those long, statuesque legs. "I mean that, if a clandestine operation wanted to hide something, they might think of working with another clandestine operation to accomplish it. Help each other out, you know?"

"I don't buy that. In any event, I need to go back through the old files, all of them, and I hate it with a passion. Where are they?"

Chapter 13

Detroit, Michigan, 2006

The two-story brownstone is one of many reminiscent of the 1920s, or earlier days, that line the whole block of this almost deserted section of town. The buildings in this particular section have seen better days and now serve as both low-rent residential dwellings and offices with many empty units in between. Maybe it's the lack of character and the architectural plainness that have prevented developers and entrepreneurs from taking an interest in this area. It could well be the proximity to the equally neglected industrial area only a block or so away that keeps this neighborhood from becoming anything other then what it is: drab, gray, generally unattractive and desolate.

The gray sedan that pulls up alongside the curb in the middle of the block represents the only movement on the block.

Two dark figures enter one of the buildings and slowly walk up the steep staircase leading to the offices on the second floor. It is dusk and the only illumination comes from a low-watt light bulb dangling from an extension cord loosely hooked to a nail up high on the ceiling where a skylight once provided the necessary daytime illumination. The single bulb is not sufficient to identify the shadowy figures that are now ascending the stairs to the second floor landing, then moving to the left into another short hallway, with office entrance doors on both sides of the corridor, they slowly move toward the middle of the hallway and stop at the door with the name, "Starlight Society, Inc." painted in black letters on the matte glass window. The door is locked but an unmistakable shimmer of light can be seen through the glass behind the lettering on the door, causing one of the men to draw an automatic pistol. He holds it ready for action, while the other guardedly knocks on the door, then backs up and away from the door to hug the wall. There's no response, only silence. It's not what they had expected. While the armed man is poised and ready for any type of confrontation, the other man quickly produces a set of lock picks, professional quality used by locksmiths and law enforcement. He proceeds to work on the door lock. It proves to be an awkward procedure, working from the side of the door to avoid becoming a potential target for somebody inside. There are no sounds, no resistance that would indicate further caution.

Finally, the sound of a sliding latch. A click. A gloved hand moves to the door knob turns and twists it gently with no resistance. Silently, the door opens inward while the second man suddenly jumps into position to fire the automatic weapon into anything or anyone on the other side of the doors threshold. They are too late. They relax. Behind the antique oak desk, sitting up in a high-backed chair, is a man in a black suit, staring at the intruders with a blank and a deathly look. In the middle of his forehead there is single bullet hole from which a thin trickle of blood is seen skirting the nose, nearly reaching the lips of the man who had earlier identified himself as "Sheldon."

The silence is broken by one of the men with a low, "Shit ... We're too late," as he twists the desk lamp to fully illuminate Sheldon's pale, lifeless face.

"Good job. Couldn't have done better myself," the armed man says. With that, he grabs the desk lamp, ignoring the cord, still plugged in, and throws it violently across the room at the dead man. The room goes dark.

Chapter 14

The Guest Room

Eleanor opens the guest room door, excited to have a visitor in the middle of winter. She has someone to talk to now while her daughter, Gail, is at work. She stands to the side allowing Smith to enter .

"There are extra towels in the bathroom cabinets and please holler if you need anything. You just get a good night's sleep Mr. Smith."

"Thank you." And with that, he enters the room as Eleanor exits. It is more then he had expected, a large room built in the early 1900s, knotty pine walls with huge beams crossing the ceiling. The large log bed is set back slightly into a recess in the wall surrounded by trophy deer and fish mounts. Huge elk antler lamps adorn both night stands also made of pine logs. It is an old fashioned rustic room with all the necessary furnishings, leather cushioned armchairs, knotty pine writing desk and a massive antique wardrobe 10 feet in height. The huge window covered by heavy burgundy draw drapes faces the entrance of the establishment.

Arturo Smith releases the latches of his medium-sized aluminum suitcase lying on the huge bed. The laptop computer is of the same material color and texture as the case now lying on the bed.

Adjacent to the bathroom door there is a knotty pine desk perfect to accommodate the laptop and other small iteems contained in the aluminum case. Smith is extremely methodical with his unpacking.

The laptop is placed in the middle of the desk. Next to it, he places what appears to be a glass tube from which a silver colored flex wire attaches to the right side of the computer. Upon pushing a key on the keyboard the glass tube begins to glow from the inside in pink, red, then a dark purple. Seconds later, the tilted computer screen lights up to Smith's satisfaction. Having accomplished this task, Smith proceeds to take two six-inch tall aluminum, or stainless steel, bottles from the case and as if they were toiletry accessories, and places them on the bathroom sink top.

The computer screen now displays an image difficult to describe. It appears to be of a galaxy with hundreds of fine lines that crisscross the screen with hundred of little numbers superimposed in a three-dimensional fashion over what appears to be a star-filled sky.

As Smith moves back to the case on the bed he touches another key and the screen image rolls to a similar, but slightly different, version of the image just seen. Smith seems satisfied but does not pay much attention to the images. Satisfied that everything is in order, he disconnects the flex wire linking the glass tube from the lap top and commits the accessories back to the suitcase. Oddly enough, this maneuver does not affect the image on the computer screen.

Momentarily, Smith's attention is drawn to

the closed drapes covering the window. Standing to one side, he slightly parts the drapes to get a peek at the outside. It is a perfect view of the front of the lodge.

The entrance light from below illuminates enough of the parking area and the approach to the lodge. He is satisfied. His vehicle is parked were he left it and the snow is still falling.

Smith returns to the case taking one more item from it, before he slides the case under the bed. It is a small packet of what appears to be a folded bundle of silvery silk material. He unfolds it to become a blanket size sheet which just seems to float in the air as Smith spreads it over the bed to which he is about to retire.

Chapter 15

Eleanor and Gail Madsen have nearly finished their breakfast while Arturo Smith is sipping on his fourth cup of coffee.

Smith realizes both Eleanor and her daughter Gail are watching him. He looks at his watch, then at his hosts. "Very early this morning, I heard thunder. Is that a common occurrence?"

Gail, an attractive young lady of 23, looks at him puzzled, then chuckles. "There 's no thunder in the winter."

Eleanor cuts in. "I know exactly what Mr. Smith is talking about. It's the plows. They came at 5 o'clock sharp. And, yes, they make a lot of noise. The sound could be mistaken for thunder."

"Of course, the plows." Smith nods pretending to understand this matter of fact well. Turning to Gail, he continues. "So, tell me, Miss Gail, what do you write?"

Gail fidgets. "News, local gossip and more news ... If you want to call that writing."

"One must start somewhere. What would you write if given the opportunity?" Smith asks curiously.

"Human interest stories, people stories, compelling stuff ... you know what I mean?"

Slang words seem to throw him off balance. "I do, yes, of course, I do ... human interest stuff."

"And what kind of writing do you do Mr. Smith?"

An expected question for him. "Science and science fiction, astrological studies."

"Wow, that's neat. Really sounds exciting."

"Yep, that's what I thought, science fiction stuff. I had it right, Mr. Smith. I mean, Arturo," Eleanor adds. "I think you said mystery novels. But does it really matter?"

Gail's excitement grows. "That is so cool. You must be published. Who do you write for?"

"Several publications, but I teach as well." Smith reaches into his shirt pocket, removes a business card and hands it to Gail.

Gail proceeds to read aloud. "Executive Director Science Studies, Standford University, Surrey, England. Wow, I thought I detected a slight accent, but it's not a typical English accent, is it?"

"An international accent," Smith replies.

"That's exactly what I thought it was, an international accent," Eleanor adds while replenishing the coffee cups.

"You must travel a lot," Gail suggests.

"I do indeed, much more so elsewhere than here in your country," Smith replies.

"So, how do you like America? Have you been here long?"

"On and off. America -- a very interesting country, quite different than the European continent."

"I just had a great idea. Maybe you could be my human interest story. Wow, what a story for our readers. You must have a lot of interesting things and experiences to talk about."

Smith smiles, actually enjoying her enthusiasm. "Well, if you give me some time to do my work, maybe."

Chapter 16

Washington

Evan Kirkland's conference table is loaded with stacks of file folders and microfiche trays.

Amber is wheeling yet another file cart loaded with ring binders and top secret files with big red stamps on them into the room.

Evan shakes his head in disgust. "Why now? Thirty years and we are still in the ozone with this character. I don't understand the significance of a new effort. Just because of this yahoo and all the fuss over him."

Amber has no clue why he is rambling. "Get it off your chest, but we still have a job to do. We need to find out just what is going on."

Evan evades her question and to himself. "Must have taken on a dozen identities over all those years since I've been involved in this investigation. How in the hell do we know who he is now and what he looks like?"

Amber has pushed the file cart against the wall and now sits opposite Evan, attempting to be of serious assistance to him. "Shouldn't we find out first who is helping him and how? I would think, once we know, we could find out the rest from the Bureau."

Evan is listening, but he is on a slightly different track.   "Do you know if the Institute for Extraterrestrial Research is still in existence? You know, the group that was headed up by that college professor at Northwestern?"

"You mean, Hyneck, Alan."

"Right. He was a good man. Talked to him a lot. Unfortunately, he's no longer around. But, there was a group associated with him. Now, that would be a logical place to start because they always want to prove to the world that the government is dead wrong."

"The cover-up conspirators. Right or wrong, I know who you're talking about. Sure, they're in here somewhere." Amber shuffles the files around again.

"Let's check it out." He looks at Amber sternly.

"But, how do we know? And who says he's up there anyway? A CIA operative ..." But she was not sure. "It's all supposition right now." Amber shrugs.

"And we, like idiots, have to revisit sixty years of paperwork. For what?"

Amber smiles at Evan. "For a government paycheck, that's what."

Evan cannot help but chuckle. He's beginning to like working with Amber. She's not only a knockout, but has a great sense of humor. Above all, they have one thing in common, a considerable dislike for Washington politics and bureaucratic blunders cover-ups included.

Chapter 17

New Mexico

The Community Hall in the small town of Midwest, New Mexico hosts a long-overdue meeting of the Star Light Society. Over twenty members have assembled here at short notice to discuss the very reason of their very existence and decide what action, if any, to take over the murder of Chicago/Detroit operative Sheldon Parks.

The Society has not had an official meeting of this kind for over 25 years. Things had cooled down since its founding in 1946. Other groups, far too radical by Star Light Society standards, have sprung up since then and inflicted much damage to the movement as a whole. There are the true believers, driven by confirmed sightings and or encounters, who are guided by scientific facts, logic and common sense. Many of these, over the years, have found their way to the Star Light Society, mostly by referral, personal recommendations or through friends. Many other groups consist of charlatans, wannabes and just some outright frauds who have nothing better to do than go to the Roswell UFO festivals and party it for the sake of frivolity.

But the Star Light Society was a serious organization which, in a sense, invented the cell system for secret, clandestine activities. Operating in small groups, infiltrating agencies of high standing and corporate conglomerates all for a common cause -- the truth behind the UFO phenomenon.

The members carried a lot of secrets into the Midwest Town Hall. None of those, however, which would be shared with anyone, not even the lower echelon members of the Society. They were on a need-to-know footing. The mission was far too important to take chances.

The meeting today is one of reconfirmation of the members' bond to one another and reaffirmation of purpose, culminating in the ultimate expose of facts marked "Above Top Secret" for over half a century.

The fact that Sheldon Parks was eliminated, was the underlying proof that the battle is still raging. Yet this gathering, and business at hand, were being discussed calmly, reviewed and acted upon with the resolve to follow a plan that was conceived and put into place initially in 1947. They said a brief prayer for Sheldon Parks and that was the end of it.

Chapter 18

Washington

Evan commits a huge stack of file folders to a file cabinet as if it meant closure of at least one segment of the assignment. "This case was officially closed in July of 1994."

"But, Evan," Amber reminds him. "That was about the time everyone completely lost track of him."

Evan needs to move around the the office. He does so, pacing the floor and grinding his teeth on his pipe. "Yes, I remember that, but before '94 he had worked with a lot of people in one hell of a lot of important places -- ICBM development, Stealth, and protective force fields. I remember it well because I put together a massive report. And, damn it, I can't find it in here anywhere. Can you look for it, please?"

Amber nods and moves to the file Evan has just closed.

"I also remember," he continues, "that every damn time a project came close to completion, he disappeared ... poof, like Houdini, but then showed up as someone else in another situation."

Amber has found a file and proudly spreads out a series of photographs on Evan's desk. "I am getting something from these. What do you see?"

Evan reluctantly looks at the photographs. "Maybe I have been at this too long. OK, detective

Amber, let's hear it?

"All the men are about the same age, right?" She picks up another file and opens it. "But the projects and photos are dated."

Evan is getting tired, grumpy and impatient. "Get to the point, Shatzie."

Amber stops, looks at him with a questioning smile. "Shatzie? where in the hell did you get that? Are you talking to me?"

Evan smiles now. "Yeah. I thought it's an appropriate nickname for you. Oh, it's meant to be complementary. Just thought it fits you. You don't mind, do you?"

Amber smiles at him. "Well, thank you, Evan. It's German for 'dear one', right?"

"Something like that. It just came to mind and seems to suit you."

"Well, if it turns you on, be my guest, Professor. That's my nickname for you and now maybe you can pay attention to the pictures."

"All right, what do you have there?"

Amber picks up a photograph with a caption that reads "1952", another photo in an Aircraft Manufacturing plant with a date of 1964. Then, another one at NASA with Werner von Braun, dated 1969, and so on. She throws the rest of the pictures back on the desk. Closing with, "Here is one from 1989. Our subject does not seem to have aged, but his look and identity change."

"You made your point. I don't know were this is all leading to but maybe give Burke at the Bureau

a call. We're not going to solve this in these surroundings.

As Amber is ready to leave for her office she
turns toward Evan. "You wouldn't want to recom-
mend me to the Bureau as an agent, would you?"

"No, Schatzie, because then I would have to
muddle through all this myself. It's too much for one
man. "

"I figured as much." Amber leaves, slightly
disappointed.

Chapter 19

The Lodge

Eleanor and her daughter are having break-fast, as they do most mornings before Gail rushes out to her newspaper job.

Eleanor needs to know. "So, what do you think of our guest, Arturo?"

"I like him, but there is something strange about him. I can't put my finger on it." She finishes her light breakfast of toasted muffins and coffee. "Where is he? Doesn't he eat breakfast?"

"Not a bite. I offered but he wanted to take a walk in town. Can't blame him for that."

Gail is curious. "How did he pick us to stay with, anyway?"

"Somebody called for him and made a reser-vation. It was a woman. Maybe somebody from that University. I mean, let's face it, there's no Holiday Inn or Best Western to pick from within a hundred miles. So, why not us?"

It did make some sense to Gail as she shrugs it off. her curiosity, at least for the time being would have to wait. She stands, grabs her coat and purse and quickly moves out the door and only mumbles, "Continental accent. Hmm? What the hell is that?"

Chapter 20

The sign proclaims "Dean's Antiques". Smith, dressed as he was when he arrived at the lodge, enters the shop and begins to browse.

Behind the shelves of collectables, junk and antiques. There is a small desk. Behind it sits the proud owner of the establishment, Dean himself. He is busy examining coins and other small items with the help of a large magnifying glass. Dean fits seamlessly in his own shop -- an antique in his own right. He is a disheveled and unkempt old man whose hair looks like he put his finger into a live electrical socket. His eyes bulge a bit above the spectacles that have slid down almost to the tip of his nose. What keeps them up there, nobody really knows.

"Can I help you, sir " he intones as he notices Smith wandering around.

Not even knowing if the question was meant for him, Smith turns and politely replies, "No, thank you."

Dean shrugs. "Feel free to look around. Prices are negotiable."

Smith is doing exactly that, looking around, until his eyes are attracted by a display of mineral specimens and metals indigenous to the geographical area he is visiting. His attention is drawn to a normally non-distinctive piece of metal resembling a thin piece of concave copper in it's natural form covered with dirt and grime. He picks it up. It's heavy. Nevertheless, he gently brushes off some of the dirt that has collected on it, causing the edge of the chunk to reveal a reddish shine.

Taking a considerable interest in the piece, he walks toward the desk and the proprietor.

Before Smith can say anything, Dean looks up at him and shakes his head.

"That's not for sale. No sirree. That is not for sale."

Smith is taken aback.

"Sorry, sir. Can't sell it. It's real special."

"Oh?"

"Now look, you might think I'm crazy, but you're a stranger, so it don't matter anyway."

"Of course," Smith agrees.

The old man continues. "Know what this is? Girlfriend of mine brought it to me and it's a secret."

"A secret." Smith nods.

"She saw it fly off that thing with her own eyes."

"Thing?" Smith is curious.

"Landed right in her backyard. Yep, came straight from a flying saucer. Lots of folks saw it. But Ethel, she ain't no kook. Saw what you're holding come right down from it. That flying saucer I mean." The old man leans forward and closer to Smith now, as if to reveal a bigger secret. "Let me tell ya, we had lots of them UFOs around here and that's no bull either."

Smith nods and repeats. "No bull."

"That's right, no bullshit. This here piece is rightfrom a UFO. A real UFO. Anyone don't believe it, can talk to Ethel. She's a real down-to-earth soul. Wouldn't lie to nobody. Know what I mean?" He then proceeds to take the piece from Smith and begins to rub violently on the rounded side of it. His effort produces a shine and some markings become slightly visible but are indecipherable. He shows it to Smith, who curiously glances at it. "That's why I can't sell it, see? No way. Ethel would never forgive me. I promised I would keep it for her. We are kind of sweet on each other. Know what I mean?"

Smith is a little dumbfounded yet curious. What he has seen and touched struck a nerve within him. But at the moment, pursuing any dialogue, or attempting to obtain the item, seems fruitless. He decides to see what the rest of the small village of Light Struck has to offer.

Chapter 21

Eleanor enters the guest room. She simply forgot to clean the room and make the bed earlier. She heads to the bed to change the sheets when she realizes that the bed is fully made. Either Mr. Smith did it himself, or he simply did not sleep in it. Puzzled by this, she moves to the bathroom finding the bathroom in clean and untouched condition. She also notices the absence of toiletries on the countertop. She fingers the neatly folded fresh towels on the racks. Just the way she had left them the morning before Smith arrived. What a strange man this Mr. Arturo Smith is. Or, what's wrong here? she thinks to herself.

Her mind races. She is slightly confused. Or is she wasting her time trying to make something out of nothing? She has not met nor heard of the perfect man, if there is such a thing.

As she moves back into the room, ready to leave, she almost does not notice the small silver laptop computer that's lies closed on the knotty pine writing desk. Curiosity gets the best of her. She attempts to open it but it does not unfold. She picks up the little unit. There is not a single port, in or out, or sign of any such thing to be seen. This is beyond her and she just cannot cope with these details right now. She checks her watch and decides to leave well enough alone.

Chapter 22

The living room is huge. At one time, before some remodeling took place, it was an extension of the great room and still has a wide and curving staircase leading to the upstairs, giving it a massive, rustic appearance. The room is tastefully decorated with a combination of rustic, old log and antique furniture. A massive leather couch and matching reclining arm chairs are placed in the center of the room around an equally massive wood slab cocktail table. Like the dining area, the room is cluttered with antiques and plants. The wall space is taken up with shelves loaded with books and an entertainment center with a large-screen television set.

Guests of the Bed & Breakfast generally used the front staircase to access their suites or rooms upstairs and had a separate clubroom upstairs with all the amenities of a luxury living area. Food, however, is always served in the downstairs dining area which is conveniently located right next to the kitchen and the private living quarters for Eleanor and Gail. It is however, not unusual for guests to be invited to use the private living room facilities when either Eleanor or Gail are present and are serving tea or coffee.

In the few years in which the Bed & Breakfast has been in operation most guests were returning seasonal customers who have become friends and are treated like family.

Currently, Eleanor is descending the stairs into the living room when Smith appears in the hallway.

"Well, hello, Mr. Smith. Just in time for lunch. Tuna salad sandwiches." While Smith follows her to the dining area, Eleanor continues. "Did you have a good time in town?   What little there is of it."

"Yes, thank you. A good time."

"Gail loves tuna sandwiches and she may come home for lunch. How about it?"

"No, thank you, but, maybe some coffee," Smith replies.

"You are such an easy guest to please. Please, make yourself comfortable and I'll be right back with the brew." Eleanor is nervous. She doesn't know why, but the condition of the guest room is unsettling to her. Not to mention the computer gadget, which has her very confused. She rushes off into the kitchen while Smith walks around the living room. Impressed with the decor, he walks to one of the many bookshelves, looking at the titles. Eleanor enters with a large tray holding the coffee pot and all condiment trays. She places it on the large cocktail table. Finally, she seats herself opposite Smith.

"What and when do you eat, Mr. Smith?   I mean, Arturo."

"A good question. I am experimenting with a new, what you may refer to as a high-potency, low-calorie, herbal diet. It cleanses the system and is very satisfying."

She pours the coffee and is, to say the least,

befuddled. Nevertheless, she adds milk and sugar to her coffee. "Well," she says. "That certainly explains why you haven't eaten anything. So, how long do you stay on this special diet?"

"A week or two is normal."

She reaches for a cigarette from a pack lying on the table. "Do you mind if I smoke?"

"No, not at all. It is not much different than the desire for caffeine. So, what do the cigarettes do for you?"

Eleanor lights her Capri. "You know, now that you ask, I know it's a bad habit and all that but I guess they help me relax."

"They do not bother me, but it seems smoking is the center of considerable controversy today."

"You can say that again. Pretty soon in this country one won't be able to smoke anywhere, anymore. Of course that can be said about some of the rest of our personal rights, as well. And I don't for a minute buy that second hand smoke stuff. What do you think?"

Smith smiles faintly. "Yes, the entire matter does seem quite strange to a stranger. I was in your State of California once. The, so-to-say, nonsmokers, had no difficulties at all in jogging in an atmosphere with severe air pollution emanating from your vehicle exhaust systems. Quite contradictory to the no smoking efforts. Would you not agree?"

Eleanor suddenly realizes that Arturo Smith seems to have all the right answers. He must be well-educated and certainly he is very charming. "Exactly my sentiments."

"Of course, the very same vehicles are also the cause of the energy crisis."

"I don't understand." She looks at him and waits for more.

"I have noticed that this is the only country on earth which does not promote or extend its resources to provide appropriate mass transport systems. A pity."

Eleanor is all ear. "It is interesting to get another point of view on things. Not that we can do or change anything about the world problems."

"While matters may seem hopeless, there is always hope. If there is a common problem as well as a common goal, people, all human beings, have the ability to bring about change."

"Sounds easier said then done."

"That depends on knowledge and wisdom. Knowledge comes from education and experiences. Wisdom comes from a higher power. All humans have the ability to do the right thing, but they must connect."

Eleanor is more than slightly overwhelmed. "You are loosing me. Connect?"

"First to thyself. Then with the intellect. And then with the greater power. This is universal."

Boldly Eleanor follows up on the topic, clearing the smoke with her hand. "So, how do we solve the problems of the world then, as silly as that may sound?"

"The world? Or do you mean the earth? I

would think that one first must recognize the problems on earth. The universe, or the world, as you refer to it, is another matter."

If Eleanor loved conversing before, she is hooked on this one. "The world, the earth ... What's the difference?"

"However you wish. Where shall we start: education, politics, nuclear energy, energy as a whole, the space program, making war, overpopulation, the food supply, not to mention water, and diseases? "Which, of all of these, is most important?"

"You're opening up a real can of worms."

Chapter 23

Gail's office is not only small but it's a mess. Her computer desk and the utility desk space extension make up her primary work area. The rest of the room is furnished with narrow tables and book-shelves, all of which are loaded with stacks of bound and unbound back issues of newspapers, clippings and related reference materials.

Whatever newsworthy events occur within a 50-mile radius of Light Struck is Gail's responsibility, everything from births to funerals, education, birth-days, retirements, politics and celebrations. When there is little or nothing to report, she manages to squeeze in some human-interest items, writing about people whose talents or activities provide unique material for good reading.

Gail is responsible only to her editor, the aging owner of the Light Struck Weekly, who is more of a mentor to her than a boss.

Gail is intelligent and a hardworking young lady, always pleasant, well-mannered and, most of all, very inquisitive. She is learning the trade from an old professional and soaking it up with great hopes to someday being discovered by a major metropolitan paper.

Right now, a personal matter needs attention. The business card Mr. Smith has given her, is scotch-taped to the frame of her computer screen. Thus far, she has been unable to get anything on Smith or Standford University on the internet.

Mr. Smith is a most interesting individual but what the hell is a polished gentleman, which he appears to be, doing in Light Struck, UP in the middle of winter. Sure as hell, he is not doing a scientific study of snow flakes. She asks herself, *What would I, Gail Madsen do as a writer, if writing a full-blown novel?*

There is an easy answer. She would choose a tropical island with endless white sand beaches lined with palm trees. Better yet, she would fly to a Greek island like Melos, in the Aegean sea, rent a room with a balcony in one of those surf side white houses. From there, she could observe the daily activities of the local fishermen around the harbor, the people enjoying the activities of the quaint sidewalk cafes and looking out over the endless azurite sea that had no horizon. Amber realized she was playing mind games with herself. She just thought about her choices as a writer. Why then, is it so unusual or outlandish for a man to choose an isolated winter setting for his writing endeavor? What's the difference? And most of all, why should she care? He was simply another guest. Certainly she and her mother had met some real characters since they opened the lodge as a bed and breakfast.

Nevertheless, Gail was intrigued with Arturo Smith. The very least she could do is to make one phone call to a friend whom she has not talked to for a long time. Cheryl, her former college class mate and best friend, could check some things out for her.

Chapter 24

Yuma, Arizona is experiencing a hot spell and Cheryl Dexter lives in a mobile home trailer that's missing an air conditioner. It is midday already and Cheryl is not even dressed but already has a can of cold beer in her hand when the telephone rings. She pulls her silky house coat over her naked body as she rushes to the breakfast counter of the extra-wide mobile home to find the telephone, a chore in itself, the counter littered with dishes, beer cans and an assortment of papers and books. Finally the cordless phone is in her hands.

"Hello?" She listens. "Gail, what a blast, it's been ages. What's up?" She attempts to slide onto the highchair and get comfortable but her short wrap is not cooperating, exposing more of her well-endowed body, but why should she care, she is alone.

"Hold on sweetie, I'm with you. Just getting organized." She takes a sip from that fresh can of beer. "Anyway, you caught me just in time. Believe it or not, I was going to clean house before Robert gets back. He's been on the road for over a week again. Anyway, I'm all ears. What ya up too, sweetie?"

Gail is on her cell phone sitting at the computer, while operating the keyboard with one hand. She stops now to pay full attention. "Cheryl, you used to be right in there with the Society. I mean, you were connected much better then I was. I went to a lot of the meetings, but I never got close to the right people like you and Robert did. I need a little help to check out something. It's very important to me."

Cheryl is all ears now, she lights a cigarette, ready to pay attention to her friend Gail. "I've got to tell you, I've been a little out of touch with the group. I've been going on some driving assignments with Robert. Shit, we been all over the country. The last meeting we had here was over six months ago. Haven't you been in touch with anyone in the your group? You're the newspaper ace and the writer."

Gail stays right on track. "Listen Cheryl, all I need is to check up on someone. It's personal, nothing to do with my job. I don't even know if anyone in the group up here would know how to do this or what buttons to push. Write this down: Name is Arturo Smith, Standford University, Sussex, England."

Cheryl is getting more interested. "Maybe if I can get a hold of Markie, remember him? He's the only one that has access to records and what's going on right now." As an after thought, she adds, "If Robert gets a truck run up your way, we may come and visit. How's the job?

Gail is grateful for the potential help. She is getting somewhere. "All I can tell you is, if it wasn't for Mom, I'd be moving to Chicago and trying for a job with the Tribune or the Sun-Times. Anyway, if and when you ever get your duff up here, you got a place to stay."

Cheryl is ready for another beer. She stands, lights another cigarette. "That's a deal. In the mean
time, if I get anywhere with this, I'll call you right away. Take care sweetie."   She hangs up and walks to the refrigerator.

Chapter 25

Washington D.C.

The DC Diner is a reminder of the good old forties and fifties. It's an entire Pullman Railroad car, fully restored, and decorated to its original state, except that more neon lights have been added to the outside to draw attention to this already most popular late-night eatery in Washington, D.C. The interior has been graced with added comfort, emerald green velvet seats, definitely an addition to the old Pullman dining cars that would whisk rail travelers from New York to Los Angeles in luxury and the ultimate in comfort. Tiffany table lamps with beaded fringe were also added, more reminiscent of the orient express. In all, the diner's ambiance and superb food services attract the everyday passerby and Washington's elite. But it has become especially popular for those late-nighters -- office workers burning the midnight candle and, after the drinking establishments close, is frequented by workers as well as by the politicians during congressional sessions.

The DC Diner is one of Evan's favorite places, whether just for a cup of coffee, or a lunch, early dinner or a snack at 3 a.m.

At this moment, Evan is on his last bite of a toasted Italian sandwich, a house specialty consisting of layers of Genoa salami, pepperoni, feta cheese,

Mozzarella, Italian red sauce and a variety of herbs sprinkled on top. He's not quite finished when Amber walks up with a thick legal file under her arm and seats herself across from Evan in the booth.

"That was a brilliant break. The boys at the Bureau were, as usual, a little late. Instead of good background material and useful information, they found a dead man. Nice neat job." She hands Evan a picture of Sheldon with a bullet hole smack in the middle of his forehead.

Evan looks at it. Then at Amber. "Who is he?"

"Name's Sheldon Parks. Age 48. Joined the Star Light Society when he was 21 years old. Born in New Mexico. Went to school in Detroit. Other than that, he's been pretty much under the radar screen."

Evan shakes his head. "Wow. Here we go."

"What do you mean," Amber asks.

"This is good," Evan nods. "Real good, because it may be part of the puzzle, if not a lot more. The 'Star Light Society', that's the key. An old group of so called UFOlogists, flying saucer nuts. One day they are organized, then they are not." Evan smiles. "A couple of years ago they insisted on getting entrance to Area 51. They claimed we were holding live little aliens there. Got that Shatzie?"

Amber is listening. "Not yet, but in time I might get it." She pauses. "Or, should I ask, is it true?"

Evan looks at her sternly. "Is what true?"

Amber comes right back. "Holding little green aliens there?"

Evan has to be careful now. "That's for some to know and you to find out."

"Thanks for the confidence, but remember, I've been trained, not to ask too many questions. So, forget it."

"Anyway." Evan changes the subject. "Star Light Society is the possible key to what we are doing. Captain Kelly, U.S. Army, was one of the key people at Roswell. I mean, really one of a handful that knew and saw a lot. A PR officer. He later became a member, if not one of the Society's founders."

Amber fidgets. "I'm listening."

"Well, Capt. Kelly has disappeared. We know nothing of his whereabouts. The mission of the Society was to help, not Kelly, but him."

Amber has to repeat "Him?" Then quickly realizes that "him" refers to the individual, the mystery man, everyone is attempting to identify and find. "So, where do you see the connection?"

"When the Star Lighters get involved, something is up. And, of all things, they got a hold of Dan Garden."

"Who is Dan Garden?"

"A microbiologist that worked at Area 51, took a powder, and started spreading stories about his work on certain top secret projects, including encounters of a third kind, for lack of better words."

"And, you're not going to clue me in, right?"

Evan's thoughts wander in a different direction. Amber's direction. He likes Amber very much realizing, however, that, romantically speaking, he is too old for her. At the same time, he loves having her around him. She is quite a dish after all. If he was 10 or 20 years younger, he would consider proposing to her. But right now, they have a working relationship that has to be maintained -- a government business relationship. He has ignored consciously or subconsciously, the subtle signs and messages that Amber has been sending his way during their time working together.

Amber's hand is on the legal file on the table between them. He taps her hand in friendly gesture. "You know Shatzie, I'm not sure myself, at this moment, what this project is really all about. Oh, I have a few hunches, but we are bound to those damn security clearances. So, I cannot always express myself clearly. That's bad for communications as whole. However," he muses as he pulls his hand off the table, but not before tapping Amber's hand lightly. "I can see what can be done about changing your security clearance."

Chapter 26

Cheryl is on a mission. For the first time in six months her husband Robert and she are attending a Starlight Society meeting. It is being held at a friend's place of business. Mark (Markie) Berger, a certified public accountant also serves as a quasi-record keeper for the southwestern office of the Star Light Society. The cell group in Yuma, Arizona consists of only eight people, all devoted society members who know how to keep a secret, "secret."

Berger, a man in his late forties, has handled considerable amounts of communication for the Society's executive offices in New Mexico. He has been entrusted with certain archive materials and records, pertaining to the Society's confidential activities. Markie is a jovial, slightly overweight, man. He not only takes his professional CPA career very seriously, but his entrusted position as vital records keeper for the Society, and he does it with great care and pride.

Markie is not only very intelligent but extremely bright and innovative when it comes to gathering intelligence and dissecting or correlating delicate pieces of information brought to him by his superiors or other member sources.

Markie organized this particular meeting but, only after he had received repeated calls from Cheryl

begging him for a favor and to provide certain information, information he could not furnish -- not
yet,
anyway.

Word had come down from the top that something was going on, but the lid was on tight. Certain
foreign intelligent agencies were seeking certain information that not even the U.S. intelligence agencies
had available to them.

Markie was also aware of the fact that Sheldon
Parks had been assassinated. He knew that it was not
perpetrated by the FBI or the CIA. That meant more
precautions had to be taken. Everyone had to be on
high alert. Damn. Again, he could not speak freely
and openly, not even to his close friends, those present
at this gathering. Subsequently, he summed it up like
this to everyone present: "We are in the final stages
of the plan that brought us together. That's all I can
say and am going to say. There is no emergency that
exists at this moment. However, there may be some
attempted communication made by the usual inquisitive agencies to snoop and dig into our business. We
all know how they operate. "If we talk to one another,"
he said, holding his right hand cupped to his ear for
emphasis, "over the phone, you can be sure someone
is listening. I urge you to be careful what you say in
talking to other members. Cellphones are becoming
our worst enemy."

One member, a woman in her late fifties, raised
her arm and asks, "They only listen if our numbers
are on their list, right?"

Markie assures her. "Very true. Remember though, they can monitor anyone's conversation. What we don't know is which words they added to their
list that trigger their recording mechanism. The only comfort I can give you is that most, or hopefully all members that came on board after they closed Project Blue Book in 1994 are probably not on their list. The cell system, as is in existence, seems to be working. If you call me and talk to me about anything other than the weather, we will be heard by someone -- guaranteed. Precisely the reason we are here right now, in person, as a private group, eyeballing each other. When we need to talk it's person to person."

Markie then addresses Cheryl specifically. "As to your specific questions and your phone call: Best I can do is stop over at your place and see what I can come up with. In the meantime don't call your friend back until I visit with you. We meet again in 20 days."

Chapter 27

Bardo's Cafe in Light Struck is small but large enough to accommodate the need of the local populous for breakfast, coffee and lunch. Bardo's specialty is, of course, pasties. The very best in the UP. Not something Gail is into. She is sitting in the far corner booth with her mother Eleanor, having lunch.

"What's this all about Gail?"

"Can't I ask my mother out to lunch once in while? Besides, it's dead at the office and I was bored."

"I made a great tuna salad for you that better not get wasted. Arturo didn't eat again."

Gail picks up on that one. "Weird. What's with him? Don't you find him strange?"

Eleanor raises her finger to make a point. "Strange, yes, but extremely intelligent and knowledgeable."

Gail looks directly at her mother a little more sternly: "Mother, don't you think our guest is a little too strange?"

"Aren't we all?" Eleanor retorts. "Yes, he's a little different, I admit but what a mind he has."

"Mother, that's not what I'm talking about. He's a stranger after all. I kind of find him interesting too, but ..." Gail stops, waiting for a reaction.

Eleanor puts her hand on her daughter's hand. "OK, OK, I know you're concerned. I have a tiny, little, bitty confession to make."

Gail is all ears now, looking at her mother questioningly.

"Before that lady called to make Mr. Smith's reservation with us, I received a telephone call from an old friend of the family, Esther Willoughby. She lives in Nevada now. She called first and told me about a friend who was in need of a place to stay while doing some studying and writing. So, my dear, Mr. Smith's visit did not come out of the blue, so to say."

Gail breathes a sigh of relief. "Thanks for telling me but he is still a strange duck, don't you think?"

"You'll get no argument from me on that one. But so are Mr. and Mrs. Ridley who stay with us every summer."

Gail still has another question. "So, why doesn't he eat normally?"

Firmly Eleanor replies. "Because he's on a special high potency, liquid herbal diet, that's why. Lot's of people are health nuts. That's why they become anorexic. He is kind of slender, don't you think?"

"Yeah, slender and strange. Oh well." Gail is reasonably satisfied with this little chat with her mother but it does not erase all thoughts about Arturo Smith from her mind.

/

Chapter 28

An hour later, Arturo Smith is descending the stairs from his room to the downstairs hallway as Eleanor enters the house.

She simply looks at him and asks, "Coffee?"

"Thank you, why not." Smith hands her a small advertising folder. "I wonder if you could tell me more about this?"

Eleanor takes the familiar information folder from him. It is for the mystery light of the UP, the primary local tourist attraction. "I suppose you would like to go see our great phenomenon?"

"I would, indeed. What do you know about it and why is it a mystery?"

They have reached the living room and are seating themselves. Eleanor lights a cigarette. "It is, indeed, a mystery light, because nobody ever figured out what it is or where it comes from. Some claim it is caused by car headlights. But that's plain old crazy. You should see it around here in the summertime. People show up from all over the country. They stand at the very end of Robbins Pond Road and gawk at the light. It comes and goes, you know. Appears and disappears."

"What do you think it is?" Smith is quite curious and anxious to get her opinion.

"I don't know but I don't believe for a second,

it's car headlights." Eleanor rattles on. "I don't believe it's radon gas coming through a crack in the earth. And a lot of people from around the area here swear it's something from outer space."

"And you think what?"

"I kind of think it's a ghost just like the U.S. Forest Service says. A conductor for the railroad at the turn of the 19th century had an accident and lost his head. Now, he's haunting that area where the railroad tracks used to be, and is looking for his head." With conviction, Eleanor continues. "One thing is for sure, it's not car headlights. Why, that's ridiculous. I've seen it with my own eyes when there's no traffic on the road and you can't even see the road. Woods are as thick as the black forest." Suddenly, Eleanor stands and walks to the video shelf next to the television set, holding up a DVD case. "Why, I have it all right here, the Mystery Light video. This tells the whole story. But if you want to see and experience the light with your own eyes, no problem. Gail, or I, will be happy to take you there.

Chapter 29

It is late afternoon when Amber arrives at Evan's office. She throws another file on his desk and smiles. "Seems that agent Burke did manage to retrieve some documents from the dead man's desk."

"So the break-in was worth it after all?"

Amber crosses her arms over her chest. "How would I know. I didn't look." Her attitude and corresponding body language expressed disappointment and an 'I don't care,' attitude.

Evan digs into the file Amber has just delivered. He talks as he reads and shuffles through the files. "Good, a list of names and correspondence I haven't seen before. This is a group that has some real radicals in it. They will try and do anything to prove the government wrong at any price. Worst of all, they know damn well it was a cover-up."

Amber laughs out loud. "That's precious."

Evan looks up at her. "What the hell is so funny?"

Amber is amused as she stands and paces the floor in front of his desk. "Here we are sworn to secrecy and we admit to a cover-up." She shakes her head in disbelief. "And then, we call them, those society members, a bunch of cuckoos, nuts, radicals, conspiracy lovers and traitors. When, in fact, we are the liars and crooks. Precious, and what a bunch of bullshit." Amber walks to the far corner of the large

office, genuinely disgusted with the way things work
in Washington and in government as a whole for that
matter.

Evan knows exactly what she is saying and
what is bothering her. He cannot disagree with her.
He knows better. He knows what is true and what
is not. But, he has to play the game with everyone
so, he makes light of her remarks with a smirk on
his face. "How big is your government paycheck,
Schatzie? And, how many weeks paid vacation do
you take?"

Amber stops pacing, smiles at him and says,
with sarcasm in her voice, "Well, since you put it that
way, by all means. We must get on with our work,
our honest work no doubt and do whatever is best
for the people. Does that work for you?" She does not
expect or wait for an answer. "Shit,"I was going to be
a stewardess. How boring."

Evan has listened to her and watched her
intently. He recalls the times when he was on the
same wavelength. He knows the scenario too well. He
has never talked about his beliefs and feelings with
anyone, because it's just not part of the Washington
culture, not for those on a career track. And it really
doesn't matter what branch of government or which
agency one works for. Once you're part of the system,
you're part of the system and one takes on the color
of that milieu, like a chameleon, whatever is in fashion at the time. "I am with you, Schatzie, trust me. I
feel the same way most of the time. Remember, I've
worked for them one hell of a long time. And here is

where it's at: Five years away from retirement, I don't want to rock the boat. Get my drift?"

"Loud and clear." Amber chuckles. "You're stuck with it. You do what they want you to do. Me, I haven't a clue. I keep getting shuffled around from department to department, given to whomever needs a bright assistant. Problem is, the other expectations, if you get my drift."

Evan looks at her and smiles. Amber is determined to have the last word.

"Ask Monica. We worked together at the White House, remember? I said, 'no' and she, well that's history now."

Evan can't help smiling inwardly. He wondered how a beautiful creature like Amber managed to escaped the romantic and sexual pressures by the vultures of the Washington elite. What willpower, he thinks to himself, or is there something wrong with her? Sure as hell, it wasn't her looks.

Amber props herself into the only comfortable wooden armchair facing Evan's desk, resigning herself to the task at hand.

"So, what else is new? I am here, ready to do whatever has to be done, even though I know very little about this mission."

Evan understands her well and senses her deep frustrations but is unable to come up with an appropriate response, at least not at this moment.

Chapter 30

Robbins Pond Road is not plowed. Only a small footpath made by previous visitors leads to the area where the road is barricaded. From there one can go no further unless on foot.

Gail and Smith, appropriately dressed for the occasion exit Gail's car and follow the narrow path first created by a snowmobile, then trampled down by boots of other curious visitors wanting to experience, first hand, the phenomenon of the mystery light of the UP.

The quarter-mile hike does not seem to affect either Gail or Smith as they arrive at the barricade closing off the road to any type of motorized traffic. To the left of the barricade is a large sign proclaiming that this is the place to view the mystery light phenomenon. Smith carefully views the sign.

Gail explains. "That's what our U.S. Forestry Department says the light is."

The sign proclaims that the light is of ghostly origin. Specifically, it claims, pursuant to the United States Forest Service, that a decapitated railroad conductor is searching for his head nightly, using a railroad lantern as he walks along the tracks. The fact that the light when it appears, does not in any way, shape or form resemble a distant railroad lantern has never occurred to anyone or, for that matter, bothered anyone, including Gail.

Smith, after reading what is on the large plague turns to Gail. "Most interesting. Do you believe in ghosts?"

"Of course, I do," Gail snaps back.

"Why?"

"Because I visited the most haunted house in America once: Summer Wind Mansion. So did my mother. Oh, yes, ghosts are real. It's a shame Summer Wind burned down a few years ago, otherwise I would take you there to experience it for yourself. Even now, what's left of it is still pretty spooky. I'll take you there if you like. It's only about fifty miles from here."

"And what did the ghost do?" Smith asks.

"What don't they do? One of the owners of Summer Wind redecorated the house beautifully. The ghost proceeded to tear all of the new wallpaper off the wall. Objects constantly moved. The china in the house was broken piece by piece. It was a mess. When we visited and were ready to leave our car wouldn't start. That happened to a lot of visitors to Summer Wind. Finally, we had to walk out over three miles to get help. It was damn scary. So, yes, I believe in ghosts."

Smith nods. "I have heard of such experiences. It seems logical to me that souls or entities after their earthly body forms have become useless, must go somewhere. Perhaps the soul's mission was incomplete while in earthly form."

Gail is intrigued and in total agreement. "You put that quite well, Mr. Smith. We've got to talk about this some more." Almost ready to turn and leave, she catches a glimmer of the light. "There is the light now." Gail points into the far distance past the barricade.

Both stand in silence now observing the phenomenon that draws thousands of tourists into the northern wilderness area. As the last shades of daylight are fading to dusk, the light is clearly visible in the far distance and seems to be at the very far northern end of the road they are standing on.

Gail explains. "It gets much brighter. And I have seen it coming straight toward me getting bigger and brighter. Then, sometimes it splits into two or more lights and vibrates." She could rattle on and tell him more.

Smith has observed the mystery light with interest and now turns, having seen the location and the so-called phenomenon him self. "An interesting experience. Thank you very much for taking me."

"No problem. I love coming out here and watching. I prefer the summer to this though."

As they turn and retrace their steps back to Gail's sedan, parked along the shoulder of the main highway U.S. 45, neither of them notice a dark blue sedan parked a few hundred feet down the main road parked in a driveway with just the nose sticking out. It would also be too far for them to see the many antennas protruding from the roof of the blue sedan. It is not until Gail's vehicle begins to move north that the blue sedan turns on its headlights and moves north too, keeping a substantial distance between them.

Chapter 31

Arturo Smith unfolds his laptop computer and connects a thin, steel wire to a seven- inch high glass tube with a round glass ball on the very top of it. The screen is blank. Only a silvery shimmer emanates from it. His fingers fly over the keyboard, which resembles no other laptop. The keys bear no markings of any kind. They are round and simply not identifiable, lacking numbers, letters or symbols, as one would expect to see on any other laptops. As his fingers expertly move across the board nothing happens on the screen, but the glass tube standing to the right of it begins to glow a light green color as it gradually transforms to dark green, blue, magenta and purple, while the ball on top of the tube glows a fiery red. Only now that the bulbous top glows red does the image on the screen changes to what appears to be a three-dimensional view of a star-filled night sky. It is a stationary view until Arturo's little finger touches a key to the far lower left of the keyboard. Suddenly, motion is activated and, like a zoom effect at the speed of light, it appears to pass the eye as viewed from a cockpit of a supersonic jet, except much faster.

Any teenage video game entrepreneur would call this the ultimate interactive action digital game technology. As suddenly as the journey into the universal void is over, the screen goes black for a split second followed by a brilliant bright green display of symbols and what seem to be numbers appears. Arturo has reached his destination and is obtaining the result he has sought.

His fingers move over the keyboard again. One thin line of symbols separates itself from the other hundred similar rows and pulsates. Arturo has found what he was after. He punches another key. The computer screen goes black, corresponding with a high-pitched beep. Indecipherable symbols appear on the screen in large lettering. Another touch on the keyboard and a roll on the screen shows the letters easily readable, appearing for a split second before the roll on the screen stops and shows a satellite image of a geographical land mass on earth. Arturo pushes several more keys. A satellite view of the Great Lakes of the United States appears. Then, just at the edge of what appears to be Lake Superior, a blue light glows and flickers. Arturo Smith is satisfied.

Chapter 32

Amber's townhouse apartment seems almost too large and spacious for one person to occupy. But thus far Amber has avoided sharing her space with any partner. Male or female. Almost 10 years in Washington made her grow up and mature fast. It was everything she expected it to be, at first that is. When she came to the capital as a legal secretary, computer savvy, a speed typist and even a better researcher. She got the right jobs, with the right people, because she had what many people her age don't have: patience, coupled with a curious mind.

She would rather spend her time in the national archive reading this and that, than at the corner pub or sports bar milling around with a beer in her hand. Every time she had made friends and partaken in the social activities with coworkers, political acquaintances or peers, she ended up with propositions she did not want to pursue. Amber is different all right.

Looking at her well-endowed, hourglass figure and her evenly molded face, one wouldn't see her as a bookworm and library buff. She may look like a Dallas Cowboys cheerleader but in Amber was a demure, studious, highly intelligent woman who had somehow managed to stay out of strange beds and destructive relationships. She'd had her share of pats on the ass and propositions, but preferred mature and intellectual relationships. At this moment, even with her disappointments over the ways of government, she liked her assignment with Evan and their current project. Even though she is just shuffling papers around, playing secretary, and as a research assistant, this job is intriguing, and top secret.

She just couldn't figure out why in the hell the government puts a lid on everything that has to do with UFOs. *So what if they are real?* Even though she has not personally seen anything even resembling a UFO, she does know people who claim, on their lives, that they has seen them. *So What?* She'd always thought. *This is a big universe. Why could there not be other life forms out there besides us little, insignificant earthling creatures?*

What she has done, since she was assigned to work with Evan, having only a hint of what it was all about, was her homework. Having access to some classified material and archives, Amber has spent several days educating herself on Project Blue Book, its investigation and conclusions. In the process of getting herself thoroughly informed, she also found tidbits of information about other events most people know little or nothing about. That's the kind of stuff she would like to know more of and the one who knows more than anyone is Evan.

For this reason she has invited Evan over for dinner tonight, into her personal and private domain. She likes Evan -- a lot -- even though he is almost old enough to be her father. He is in some ways very much like her -- a researcher, a bookworm, studious and had an inquiring mind, just like her. She often thought that is Evan would shorten his hair, shave and dress

sharply, he would look more like a distinguished
gentleman professor or statesman rather then the mad
scientist he appears to be at times.

She does not have much time to carry her
thoughts further, applying the final touches to the
table setting for a dinner for two. Having done that,
she examines the overall effect. For some strange reason that she cannot explain even to herself, she is taking extra care to make a good impression on Evan.

It is a cozy, contemporary setting created by
a mix of furnishings, wall decorations and intricate,
indirect lighting. It is easy to see what dominates
Amber's time off duty, her townhouse apartment. Her
apartment is her research nook. Her Sanctuary. Just
as she returns to the kitchenette breakfast counter to
check on the salad mix. The doorbell rings. *Why am I
fussing?* Instinctively, she looks at herself in the recep-
tion area mirror before reaching to open the door.

The view catches her by surprise. The man
standing under the arch of the open door frame is
Evan all right but not the same guy she is used to
seeing at work in the Pentagon offices. His normally
bearded, unshaven appearance, has yielded to a culti-
vated, well-groomed van dyke and neatly combed full
head of hair.

"Evan?" Amber asks quietly.

He shrugs and smiles. "It's me."

Chapter 33

With only the parking lights on, the maroon sedan moves up the driveway leading to the Bed & Breakfast. The dark, tinted windows reveal nothing of the interior. Only the almost unnoticeable short wire antennas protruding from the top of the sedan are suspect and would raise the eyebrows of a knowledgeable observer. The sedan keeps a cautious distance from the entrance. It stops, backs up in the large parking area and, as if having observed enough, moves away from the lodge.

Somebody has observed this silent activity from a second floor window of the lodge, judging from the movement of the drapes, now drawn shut.

Chapter 34

In Eleanor's living room, the telephone rings. "Hello," Eleanor answers the portable speaker phone.

"Mark here," booms the voice on the other end. "How are things going?"

"Fine, I think," Eleanor answers with a sense of curiosity.

"What's Gail doing?"

There is a moment of silence as Eleanor picks up the receiver and paces the length of the living room floor, then asks, "Why? What's the matter?"

"Everythings fine so far but there is a lot of chatter. Gail talked to Cheryl and we had a meeting. She's curious about Smith. She doesn't know, does she?"

"Of course not, Mark," Eleanor answers with conviction. "But she is the curious type, you know. For that matter, so am. I love talking to him. Trivial stuff, ya know? He's such an interesting individual."

"Well, just keep things status quo on your end. Cheryl will talk to Gail. And we are doing what we have to do. Will talk later, bye," Mark replies firmly.

Eleanor commits the telephone to a receiver on a small, roll-top desk in the corner of the room and closes the roll-top's lid.

Chapter 35

Evan and Amber are sitting opposite each other at the dining table. They have finished eating and Amber is refilling Evan's teacup with more orange pekoe tea. He asked for that particular flavor several times at the office, and Amber remembered, going out of her way to make sure she would have some for this evening.

There are two reason why Amber invited Evan over for dinner to her very private sanctuary. One, to talk about her research completed since she's been on this assignment. The other, a little more personal. She wants to know what makes Evan tick? Or is it more? Sure as hell, she did not expect Evan to look the way he does now -- a clean-cut, well-groomed gentlemen.

Sipping on his tea, he starts the conversation. "I am impressed, if not overwhelmed, by your culinary talents,.thank you. It was excellent. I had no idea." He pauses.

"That what?" Amber smiles and continues. "That I could cook? Part of my conservative Wisconsin upbringing. I'm glad you enjoyed it. And, it's certainly a change from the Washington Diner, I thought."

"They don't make schnitzel like you do. That was just awesome," he exclaims with true enthusiasm.

"Seems we are in good shape then," Amber replies and changes the subject. "Now, Evan, let's get serious. What do you know about Aurora?"

Evan leans back and looks at her, a little surprised. "Aurora? Aurora what?"

"Texas, 1898 - that Aurora. You know what I 'm talking about."

"You have been reading the old files, haven't you?" Amber nods, and Evan knows there is no escaping it. "OK, there's no harm in it. That's not classified anymore. I know what you're getting at. Of course, it was a cover-up, all the way. Then, lucky for the powers that be, people just forgot about it. Why are you digging into that?"

Amber is determined. "Because I am curious about everything I could find in the old file. All information ends with some UFOlogist finding out about the crash and the body. It's public record now. An unidentified flying object crashed in Texas and an alien body was found and buried by the townsfolk of the little town. Hundreds of people saw it . Even more people attended the funeral."

Evan is watching Amber intently. He has to interrupt. "I know the whole story, Schatzie. It happened in 1898. It was a different world then. There were no flying saucers, UFOs and, sure as hell, no media mania to spread that kind of stuff. Got it?" He continues. "Then, beginning in the 1920s and all the way through the early 1940s, the forerunners of today's UFOlogists and space nuts, whatever you want to call them, tried to exhume the body of whatever it was those people buried in that little village which, by the way, could have been simply nothing."

Amber is watching Evan closely. A smile comes to her face as she thinks, *Evan is so good at this game, so convincing when he does his tap dance routine to avoid the truth. He has a way of simply putting a lid on things at some point in the conversation.* She smiles because she can look right through him.

Evan notices this. She is different. Is it something personal, Evan ponders? Deep inside he knows that he just cannot put something over on her. "Just why are you so interested. What's the big deal? It's all old stuff."

Amber stands up and begins with her usual pacing, characteristic to her queries or attempts to make a point. Whenever she does this her tight skirt accentuates her thin waistline and round and very firm contoured butt that sways just too nicely from one side to the other in front of Evan. He forces himself to look into her eyes. "Evan," she begins. "We've been given a job to do, of which you know a lot, and I know way less. I would like to know where this is all going. To do that, I have to try to educate myself. I have access to lots of files. Interesting ones at that. I am getting a feel for how things get handled and treated. I also noticed the disappearance of reference materials that are supposed to be there, but then they are not. So? Where in the hell are these documents? The conclusions to everything?" She is upset now. "Evan, I am good at research. I know my job. I am given access to complete project files, except that some pages are missing. The most important pages. The proof. Gone. And I bet that there is another file somewhere that's above the above top secret file. Right?" Now, she looks straight at Evan, truly hoping for a straight answer from him.

Evan nods his head in submission to her question. "Of course, there is. There's always another file and bits of information that get shuffled upward. And whatever that is, it stays up there. Just like you said, it ends up in some other above-top-secret file, and, you think, I have access to it?" Evan shakes his head with conviction. "Forget it. I am not one of those privileged ones. And, if I was, I couldn't tell you anything anyway. Why do you have this passion to dig in so deep?"

"Now that's an easy question to answer." Amber sits down at the table and faces Evan. "I just want to know what we are doing. What is it that we have to accomplish? Why is everybody so uptight and curious about the whereabouts of Mr. No-Name?"

Now Evan stands. He is a little nervous, or maybe shy. "Amber," he says. "There is a reason why I had to straighten out my act, so to say." He gestures to his attire, his haircut and his trimmed beard with both hands. "I was informed this afternoon that the president want's to talk to me."

Amber looks at him with surprise and a certain disappointment. She had, for more then a minute, thought that Evan had gone through this physical transformation because of her and her carefully planned dinner invitation. Nevertheless, she is impressed with both Evan's new look and the news about his presidential meeting. Something must be up and, irrespective of her ongoing doubts, there is a tingle of excitement in her.

Chapter 36

Eleanor and Smith engaged in casual conversation in the Lodge's living room -- idle conversation. The television set is on, providing the usual repetition of newscasts, the same mix of bad news, trivia and commentaries, heard daily around the clock. Smith seems to be aware of the routine and, while he glances at the screen, he seems more amused by what he sees and hears than affected by it.

Eleanor on the other hand watches television every chance she gets, which is most of the time. She is profoundly affected by everything from news, politics, commentaries, gossip and to the tabloid nonsense. In between, she watches the soap operas and whatever game show she can find on the cable menu. She is quick to take a stand on political issues but does not cross the line for either party because she is a middle of the road independent and as confused as most people in America about what is right or what is wrong. She has often wondered, though, why there are so many Americans that take the ostrich, head-in-the-sand approach to everything. She's not radical in any sense, just old fashioned, stubborn, mildly set in her ways and wondering what happened to the good old days of the fifties and sixties when life seemed much simpler, friendlier, with less government, fewer regulations and more opportunities. Eleanor definitely is a curious individual ready to listen and observe with interest on a wide variety of subjects. Simply, she is open-minded and loves to learn more. In all, as reclusive and unworldly as Eleanor is taken by some people sometimes she can be quite an actress and a diplomat. After all, she has put up with different types of guests during the high season.

She caters to her guests and does a good job of it, attempting to understand their realities and their worlds. That's what pleasing people is all about. She firmly believes that.

Now, with Mr. Smith, it is a slightly different story. She has some real problems, the kind of problems she can't talk about, not even to her daughter Gail, who in many ways is much like her mother and her grandmother, for that matter.

But, it's Mr. Smith who is on her mind. She likes him very much but doesn't know exactly what to make of him. She has some feelings that frustrate her. Her mind flashes back to the time when an old friend, Theresa Summers, called her to make the reservation for him. Eleanor was perplexed, even confused, maybe because Theresa didn't tell her everything she should know. Why would anyone come to Light Struck in the UP of Michigan in the middle of winter? Yet alone to a remote Bed & Breakfast with not much going for it, especially out of season. She does get calls in the wintertime from snowmobilers needing accommodations. As a matter of fact, she had inquired of Theresa if Smith was a snowmobiler or maybe a skier. But no, Theresa had said. *He's just a gentleman that needs some peace and quiet to do some of his research.*

So, Eleanor had acquiesced to the request from an old friend. Why should she care anyway? Eighty-five dollars a day, prepaid is nothing to ignore during the off season.

Once she had met Arturo she was and, still is, quite impressed with her visitor, a worldly, polished gentleman who, as it turned out, is an excellent conversationalist, smart, pleasant and makes for very nice company. Gail, too, made a bit of a fuss over this unusual winter visitor at first but then yielded to her mother's decision and simply went along with it. What, then, is this gnawing, uncomfortable feeling in her stomach that just sits there like having eaten a greasy duck dinner. Or is it all in her head? She is not about to trouble herself with these feelings. It will all work itself out. Period.

Smith in the meantime, instinctively knows he has to move faster and take advantage of every bit of time necessary to accomplish what needs to be done. At the same time, he must maintain a good personal relationship with both Eleanor and Gail to accomplish what needs yet to be accomplished.

Chapter 37

Gail is in her office when Cheryl calls.

"Sorry it took so long," she apologizes. "We managed to attend a meeting and I had a chance to talk to Markie about your situation."

Gail is all ears. "What did you find out?"

"Well, on the specific information you wanted, there's no such university as Standford. But, there is Stanford of course. Shit, and do you know how many Smiths there are in England? Give me a break here."

Gail is not just disappointed, she is a little worried. "OK, OK, I get it. But what about Arturo, that sure as hell is not a common, everyday name?"

"Just keep your shirt on, or whatever your waltzing around in," Cheryl replies with her usual sense of off the wall humor. "Most of all, keep your cool. What phone are you using -- home, your cell or office?"

"Why?" Gail snaps back.

"Never mind, just tell me," Cheryl demands.

"I'm on my cellphone."

"Good. Don't worry about your Mr. Smith, OK? He's a friend of our friends. I think something sucks. Whoever came up with that bullshit cover story is losing it. Just don't ask me for any details, because I don't know any. What I can tell you is that something big is going on and I am sure your guy is part of it," Cheryl rambles on. "I've been with the group now for over 15 years and we had meetings every year or so. Now, all of a sudden, everybody is calling everybody and I hear there are meetings all over the damn place every time the phone rings. What 's up? I don't know, because nobody is telling me anything and believe me I would love to know.

Gail is all ears but not happy with the information which, to her, is no information. "That's a fine how-do-you-do. What the hell am I supposed to do with all of that?"

"Don't you freak out on me or get too nosy. There must be a damn good reason for the hush. But I'll find out more and I promise I'll pass it on to you."

"One more question about him staying with us. Is there anything we should worry about?"

"What are you talking about? Of course not but one more thing. Don't tell your mother we talked. Bye sweetie." The line goes dead.

Gail appreciates the info, but is angry, too, for not receiving more. Gail is intelligent and level-headed. *What do they think? She can't keep a secret?* She became a member of the Star Light Society when she was in college. The organization was one of young and old people then who simply believed that there was life on other planets. Many of the members were amateur astronomers, sky searchers, they called themselves. Many were just believers that unidentified flying objects were real. Many of her member friends had actually seen UFOs and, at various meetings of the local chapter of the society, would share their experiences with the rest of the group.

She also remembered simple pajama parties when they would talk about close encounters of the third kind, sightings and just stuff that would compare to an evening among friends sharing and scaring themselves with good Ghost Stories.

There was the cover-up thing, the word constantly popping up, always in the same breath with the word "government". It was precisely the talk about government cover-ups that made belonging to the Star Light Society exciting and gave the Society validity.

She also realized that if the government would not have made such a fuss about covering up any UFO sighting the society as a whole would not have had such a strong bond and heightened desire to expose such cover-ups. One thing she was sure of: Ninety percent of her friends and acquaintances firmly believed that government UFO cover-ups were a fact.

Gail could never figure out what was so important for Uncle Sam to hide the truth from the people. Whenever she inquired about this with senior members of the Society she was told that several governments are always in a race to obtain technological information from any crashed UFOs. She had heard about the Siberian crash of a saucer and found that communist Russia covered up everything. Oh a few photographs sneaked out, but that's it. She had to smile thinking of that.

Are we, in America, any better or different than other governments? Hell, no, she concluded. There is no difference. Put a lid on everything you don't want the people to know and cover it up.

Gail has not been active in the Society for over 10 years. There are no chapters, or members that she knows of, nearby. The last contact with everyone she knows or knew was when she went to the Roswell UFO Festival over a year ago, mostly for the fun of it. Thinking back on that experience, she felt mixed emotions. There were some serious people there but also a lot of nut cases who give the true UFOlogist a bad name. It was like Halloween and ghosts. There are a lot of Halloween nuts, but how many have had real experiences involving ghosts, poltergeists or haunted houses? Probably only a very small portion of all those making a big thing out of Halloween.

For now, Gail was going to go along with whatever was going on and see what transpired. She liked Arturo Smith. He is a good guy, a friend of a friend, and part of something important. Gail was sure she would get more information from Cheryl. She turns back to her computer to write another meaningless trivia piece for her paper.

Chapter 38

Jason Roberts has become a very busy man all of a sudden. He is in his darkroom carefully preparing an entire series with duplicates of close up photographs of what he captured through his telescope on July 2, 1947. Before entering the darkroom, he had secured his house and checked every lock three times -- the front door, the back door and the garage door. Every one had a dead bolt in addition to the regular door locks. Then, and only then, had he opened the safe tucked away in a basement corner and camouflaged with halved banana boxes. All his precious negatives had been stored in there for years, except for those copies he had faithfully delivered to the Star Light Society.

Suddenly, within the last few weeks his phone has been ringing off the hook with requests from old friends and Star Light members to produce sectional close-ups of the original photographs. What he is working on may well be the only evidence in existence of exactly what had happened and what caused that phenomenon at Roswell in July of 1947. Dozens of prints were hanging on his darkroom wash line drying. With his huge magnifying glass, he strained to see the detail on the hanging prints. He was not satisfied. He shakes his head. He would have to take the negatives and scan them into the computer. That would make a difference, he thought.

Quickly he takes a strip of negatives, turns off the red darkroom light and exits the dark room, rushing to his computer in the adjacent office. Computers have been the solution to many of his efforts for years now, but he never gave the old negatives a second thought, especially since, after the entire Roswell matter was debunked by the government as a weather balloon story. While he knew better, he was not going to get involved then, other than to do whatever he could for his friends at the Society. Now, he placed the negatives into a frame tray, let it slide into place to scan and convert the negatives into positive images on the computer screen. Wow. He had almost forgotten how unique they were.

Jason now has the images on his desktop, carefully placing them in a downward trajectory until seven images of the saucer-shaped object are neatly arranged on the screen from right to left, downward. But it is not until he enlarges the master shot, with all seven discs in place, that he notices something he had simply not seen before. He also had to wonder if closer perusal by some of the scientific experts at the Society had discovered more detail then he had initially and for that reason they had asked him to do this detail chore for them.

The image in the upper right hand corner of the screen, the first frame that had captured the object as it came into view, is nearly a clear image of a disk-like spacecraft. Better yet, it looked like two dinner plates upside down, pressed together. A large, half-sphere bubble protruded from the top and a much smaller sphere protruding from the bottom of the craft. On the second photo something strange seems to have occurred on the lower part, or the underside, of the saucer-like craft. Light spots appeared, comparable to sparks from a sparkler, being emitted from the underside. The third close-up of the saucer is normal, as is the first. Finally, Jason gets to the last and smallest of the images and blows it up tenfold. Something is missing here. Very simply, the half-sphere seen on previous photos is missing.

Going back to all the images, Jason discovers that the lower sphere is missing from the photos only after the sparks appear underneath the craft.

Finally, maximum enlargement of the photo with the sparkler effect provides a clear image of a large gray object, with the contours of a half sphere in a downward, spiraling, vertical position.

Something big happened that night. Jason knows that for sure. Now, upon closer examination, there is sufficient evidence that something from the space ship separated and plummeted to earth that night only moments before the crash occurred in the desert near Roswell, New Mexico. He will commit this crucial evidence to a CD and get it to the Society Board of Directors in a hurry.

Chapter 39

Smith and Eleanor are still engaged in conversation while the television set is blaring away. The war in Iraq is still going strong and the controversy over it even bigger and stronger.

"Will this ever end?" Eleanor asks.

"I am afraid not."

"Good God, what are you saying?"

"Please, do not be upset. There is little one can do until people on this planet come to their senses which will not occur until a major disaster brings the leaders of this planet to their knees, followed by the masses."

"What a dreadful thought. Do you believe in God, Mr. Smith? I mean Arturo."

"Of course ... a universal reality."

"Well, do you really think God will let such a thing happen?"

"Only if man is not willing to change for the better. Unfortunately, there are few signs of that, as you are witnessing yourself."

"What do you mean?"

"You are being spoon-fed information through this tube here, around the clock. Most of what is transmitted to you, you take as the truth."

"You're scaring me Arturo. What do you mean?"

"You are given information to believe that

your war in Iraq has a purpose. You believe the purpose to be democracy. Freedom is the word most often
used. When, in fact, the conflict is about something
else -- power and energy."

"Of course energy and oil have a lot to do with
the whole thing. You are probably right."

Arturo smiles. "All energy sources will be
exhausted soon. Then what? Your nuclear energy will
either backfire or be misused. The excess and waste of
energy is also not helping this planet. You blame it
on a variety of things, take global warming and what
have you, all nonsense."

"Don't look at me. I'll have no part of any of
that," Eleanor states.

Arturo muses. "You have an automobile, yes?
And your daughter Gail has one too. Yes?"

"Why of course, how would we ever get
around here in the countryside without a car?"

"Precisely, their is a rational explanation for
everything. Multiplying the need plus the excess and
second car mentality are all part of the problem, if not
a primary factor in air pollution, energy consumption
and other environmental concerns you are faced with.
Not to mention these so called SUVs. Recently I was
given a ride in what is called a Hummer. Wonderful
contraption. It could be used on the moon, if one can
afford the gasoline it consumes."

"So where is the answer?" Eleanor looks at
Smith with anticipation.

"Your country, Ms. Madsen, is one of few that
does not have an even adequate mass transportation

system. America is dependent on oil. Not just its own but very much on that, of other countries. From there on, you figure it out. It boils down to simple mathematics and, of course, politics. Then, there is the next missing link. Statesmanship and leadership. The masses, because they are spoiled and preoccupied in soaking in their own fortunes, or misfortunes, will not have the capacity or the power to elect such leaders necessary to bring change. I do hope I am not frightening you. Please accept my comments above all as hopefully thought provoking."

"I do, I do, Mr. Smith. Arturo, I mean. I think there is much truth to what you have said. And believe me, I am taking it to heart."

Chapter 40

The U.S. Forest service and the county transportation department intentionally did not plow out Robbins Pond Road in the winter. They do not want to encourage more traffic to the mystery light. More traffic meant more care-taking services of the viewing site area, including garbage pickup and disposal. Unfortunately, casual visitors and tourists tended to leave something behind, the most common being beer and pop cans or plastic bottles that end up strewn about the entire area.

This winter morning, however, Robbins Pond Road was getting some attention. It was being plowed out thoroughly. Nothing about this activity was unusual. Big plows at work is an every day occurrence in the area. What was not usual, is the snow white panel van snuggled into a logging road entryway three hundred yards south of Robbins Pond Road. The van's nose pointed just far enough out toward Highway 45 for those inside to observe the parking area. The white van easily faded into the white snowy background and would remain hardly noticed were it not for the many antennas that protruded from the roof. The vehicle looked void of any driver and passengers.

Once, however, the two Gogebic County snow plows completed their job and move north on Highway 45, the white van begins to move toward Robbins Pond Road where it makes a swift left turn toward the viewing site. The van can only go as far as the metal posts cemented into the ground by the Forest Service, presumably to prevent people from going further down the road where a severe wash-out has occurred and further hinders clear passage toward the light source.

The residents of the surrounding area have accepted the fact, as: *That's just the way it is.* There is a washout, that prevented anyone from driving down the road and toward the source of the light. A few hundred feet before the washout, near the barricade, the U.S. Forest Service had placed a large, nicely engraved site marker explaining the history and pre-sumed cause of the mystery light itself.

Chapter 41

Arturo Smith has given more thought to this viewing site, as much thought as he has given to the light itself. The washout on Robbins Pond Road was from natural causes. So, it would seem. What has occurred to Smith is, Why was it not fixed? Instead, in this particular and very peculiar case, the U.S. Forest Service had made a concentrated effort to ignore fixing the washout, yet erecting instead, an expensive barricade to block passage and discourage anyone from exploring the road toward the source, what the Forest Service had officially named and claimed to be the Paulding Light.

Smith grasped this thought-provoking situation within seconds of visiting the viewing site with Gail. He had not shared these thoughts with her or Eleanor. He knew exactly what went on and why. It was a very clever move by the government to simply 'Give 'em something but, don't give 'em too much.' He knew from the moment he stood on the snow covered viewing site with Gail what was going on and that the long fingers of the American government had reached into this remote area.

This very morning as Smith manipulates his computer screen, looking at what appear to be satellite images of vast expanses of winter wilderness. Multiple magnifications reveal very thin, hardly detectable lines which Smith is carefully studying.

He does not need much more information to do what he must do. Everything is committed to memory now, except the timing is crucial to his task. Smith will also have to be absolutely sure that no one else is in the area when he makes his move. He has received no official warnings or any buzz from assisting sources that his presence in the Upper Peninsula is known. Even if that were the case, certainly his purpose would remain a secret.

He had noticed the maroon sedan when visiting the light viewing site with Gail. It could be any number of sources who have attempted to keep track of him. Generally though and lucky for him thus far, the occasional surveillance of him was more for his protection rather then his detriment. Nevertheless, he had to be careful.

Chapter 42

The white panel van pulls up to the metal road barrier. From the top of the van a one inch white pipe holding a white telescopic device moves up, then pans the area and locks in on the direction of the light source.

While the light can quite often be seen during broad daylight, it is not the case now. There is nothing to see. After a minute or so, the telescope goes down and the panel van backs up, turns around and leaves the site.

Chapter 43

Arturo Smith places the aluminum suitcase on his bed, then opens it. The case contains what appear to be layers of aluminum foil, neatly folded in small eight-by-ten inch packets, resembling neatly folded linens. His hands reach underneath and to the bottom of the suitcase. The silvery, shining pack of folded material, Smith now unfolds and forms it into a perfectly square, ten-by-ten inch container. It is a a perfect cube, stiff and solid to the touch with an equally thin, barely noticeable carrying handle on the top.

Fully satisfied with having the right packet, Smith collapses the cube container and folds it into its original flat form within seconds. He sets the refolded material to the side and adds several other folded pieces of material to the first one. He stuffs all of them into the pocket of his overcoat.

Minutes later, Smith is walking into the kitchen downstairs where Gail is having a late breakfast.

"Good morning , Miss Gail, I wonder if you could be of help to me?"

"I can try."

Smith spreads out a map of the area on the table, pointing. "This is where we went to view your mystery light, is that correct?"

Gail familiarizes herself with the map and

nods. "That's the spot all right. Planning to go back?"

"Yes, I am indeed." He leans over the map and points. "This line here, is this another road that connects to this Robbins Pond Road?"

Gail is interested and more than willing to help. "Sure, that's Sleepy Hollow Road. For sure that's snowed in and not plowed but there is a logging road just north of Robbins Pond Road that takes you to the best viewing site of the light. It's at least two hundred yards north of the barricade, right up on a high hill and just to the right of the high-line posts. It's definitely the best viewing site there is."

Smith is very interested. "If, as you say, that is the best viewing site, then why the barricade?"

"Beats me. I don't know."

"Does it make sense to you, Miss Gail, that a barricade is built were there should not be one?"

"That's because of the washout on the road. They don't want people to get stuck   there."

"Roads can be fixed, can they not?" Smith asks.

"I guess. Yeah, you're right, the road could have been fixed." Gail is thinking and looks at Arturo Smith with great curiosity. "You're right. Absolutely right. Why didn't they fix the road?" She thinks for a moment, then comes up with the logical answer. At least she thinks so. "Then people could drive all the way up Robbins Pond Road and closer to the light."

"Precisely, and they don't want that to happen."

"This is very confusing, but interesting. I have never given the washout or the barricade a second thought until you brought it up. That is an interesting question." She rattles on. "I know that the top of the hill off of the logging road is the best viewing site. I must tell you though, that a lot of people have tried walking the road to get closer to the light and found nothing. It's just like a ghost. It just disappears. So what's the difference? Nobody will ever find out what it is. A lot of people have tried."

Smith smiles. "My overwhelming curiosity is driving me to make at least a reasonable effort to try to examine this phenomenon a little closer." He takes the map folds it and turns to leave.

Gail is pouring herself another cup of coffee and impulsively calls out to Smith. "Mr. Smith, Arturo I mean, I'm just wondering," she says with considerable hesitation. "I'm just wondering," she tries again, before hesitating again. "Have you ever heard of an organization known as the Star Light Society?"

Smith reacts. There is recognition, but he does not show it. "The Star Light Society, why do your ask?"

"I thought, you being a writer of science and astronomy, you might be familiar with the name."

"The name is vaguely familiar, but difficult to place at the moment. What do you know about them?" Smith cannot help asking.

"They are a research organization."

"Research of what?" Smith has moved back into the kitchen and sits down opposite her at the kitchen table.

"Astronomy research, same kind of stuff you're into. Some people call them 'sky watchers'."

Smith is amused with her cautiousness and her curiosity. "Sky watchers? And what do they watch for?"

Finally, Gail shoots back. "Unidentified flying objects of course. UFOs you know, they like to watch the skies in the hope of life on other planets."

Smith likes Gail. He does not mind taking time out to converse with her, although there are limits to what can be discussed. "You seem to be quite familiar with them, the Society you mention. What they do. So, what do you believe? Are they an organization with a worthwhile cause?"

"Of course," Gail snaps back affirmatively. "And I find the subject matter not only fascinating, though I have yet to see a UFO with my own eyes. All I manage to observe is what turns out to be satellites circling the earth."

Smith stands ready to go, nodding to her. "With your genuine curiosity of the subject matter, I am sure you'll be seeing one of those UFOs soon." Smith walks out, leaving Gail alone with her coffee and more frustrated, so much so that she extracts a pack of cigarettes from her purse and lights one stubbornly, pouring more coffee and pouts.

Unexpectedly, Smith returns to the kitchen once more addressing Gail. "Oh, by the way, there is no Standford University, only a Stanford University in England. Just like your friend Cheryl told you." He smiles at her and leaves again.

Gail stares at him and is completely dumb-founded. How in the hell does he know about Cheryl and her conversation with Cheryl? She is completely confused and visibly upset. About what? She does not know for certain. It's just all very perplexing. Nevertheless, she is going to find out what is going on now, come hell or high water.   Her inquisitive mind cannot stand unsolved mysteries.

Chapter 44

Washington, the Pentagon

The Conference Room is one of many large meeting rooms used for Pentagon security briefings. The equally large conference table is cluttered with documents. Amber has spread out a series of files and photographs on the floor for examination. In the process, while on her knees, she does not realize that her well-rounded butt is stressing the tight miniskirt aimed at the Conference Room door, when Evan enters. He stops. Closes the door behind him quietly. He cannot help smiling while enjoying the view.

Working on a new sexercize program?" he asks casually.

Amber swings around and sits. Facing him pulling up her knees as best as the tight skirt allows. "No, it's what I do to earn my precious government salary."

Evan looks well-groomed today, dressed in a business suit, and continues to find delight in looking at Amber. "How obedient and thoughtful of you. We've got to talk."

Amber gets up and moves to the conference table. "I did plenty of work already, some homework you may not want to hear."

"Does that mean you want a raise?" Evan cannot help asking.

Amber ignores the question. "I decided to go through all the old files to get a better grip on everything we are supposed to be doing and I discovered something. All of the cover-up experts in our department and the CIA blatantly ignored which, however, may have a direct relationship to the current activities."

"OK, spare me the suspense and hit me with it."

Amber shuffles some papers around on the conference table and pushes them to the side to make room for herself and her documents. "Turn back the clock to 1947," she says as she sits opposite Evan. "Two key people, intimately involved with the affair were, one, a nosy mortician who wandered into the wrong part of the base hospital. The other was a nurse that assisted in the autopsy of one of the subjects."

"You're telling me what I already know," Evan responds with a little impatience in his voice.

"Not so fast. We were able to keep everyone in check and send out all kinds of misleading spins on the truth."

"Shatzie," Evan cuts in, "I hope this is not another one of your attempts to express your dislike for our employer."

"Evan," she comes back sternly. "There was real negligence involved here. Maybe you want to call it an oversight which, however, could come back and bite everyone involved in the proverbial ass. I mean ours, too."

"All right what is it?"

"Our great intelligence community in charge of the mess at that time neglected to take into consideration, one little thing -- a baby."

"What the hell are you talking about?" Evan bursts out.

"Yes, the baby, the one that has all the facts from the very eyewitness to the autopsy."

"Keep going."

"There was an old file in that stack." Amber turns and reaches down to the floor and picks it up. "It was unmarked and taped shut. No identification on it." She slaps it on the table. "It gets better yet. I checked subsequent files from about the time when Unsolved Mysteries first aired on network television. A witness report tried to bring this issue to the forefront, to the public, but nobody listened. Everyone involved in the show was told to shut up. Or, they were discredited." Amber again reaches down to the floor to pick up another file with a thick red tape marker on it. "Here are the whole cover-up details for that."

Evan reaches for both files, picks them up and glances inside. "OK, it's a revelation, if it's all true. How does it help us now?"

Amber is ready. "The nurse, the one that was right there during the autopsy, before she passed on, she left her diary to who else?" She pauses. "Her daughter of course. Nobody knew that she was pregnant at the time."

Evan puts the two files carefully to the right side of him on the table. "You made your point. It's a good one but, who in the hell is it and where do we look to find her? First thing you can do for me is to call Secretary Runsfeld, tell him to stall on that meeting with the President until I have a chance to look at this whole thing carefully." He stands, taking the two files, putting them under his arm. "Shit, I'm not ready to provide all the answers yet because I don't have 'em. Thanks for the work and the dinner. Loved it. We must do this again sometime. He gently gives her a kiss on the cheek and departs.

Chapter 45

The SUV Smith was driving is parked on a log-ging road so it cannot be seen from Highway 45. What appears to be the figure of Arturo is walking deep into the woods. The view is occasionally obstructed by the thickets of balsam and spruce trees standing amidst the mostly hardwood maple forest.

Chapter 46

On Robbins Pond Road, near the barricade of the mystery light viewing site, a maroon sedan with the usual antennas protruding from it's roof is parked and two men in long dark winter overcoats exit from the sedan and proceed to set up a tripod. They attach a camera with an extra-long telephoto lens to it. It is an activity that is not unusual at the viewing site. Would it not be for the antennas covering the roof of the sedan it would be just another individual or videographer attempting to get a better film, video or photo image of the mystery light to prove it's real origin or location. The other difference from all the usual camera buffs and wannabe scientists is that these two men converse in Russian. "Davai, Davai," (hurry hurry) can be heard from one of them, presumably the one in charge of the photographic session.

Chapter 47

Gail, dressed in a snowmobile suit, is struggling through the woods to get to the secondary viewing site of the mystery light situated on top of a hill. It is a secluded site that provides the best of cover, with thick elder brush and small balsam trees. But, it is also not an easy location to reach, made more difficult with the accumulation of at least 12 inches of snow packed and crusted on the surface. High drifts in some areas between trees require every bit of her strength and ability to maneuver. Holding onto her camera bag with one hand and pulling herself up another foot or so by holding on to a tree branch, she literary inches herself up to reach the top of the hill. From this tree-sheltered vantage point she can get quite a view if she can avoid or push aside the thick evergreen branches that surround her.

With determination, she connects a 12 -to-120 zoom lens to her Nikon still camera and waits for some action. She has decided that she is going to take some matters into her own hands and find out just what is going on. She knew from the time she took Smith to see the mystery light that something was up. She had wondered, as well as worried, about who Smith was and just why did he come here to visit them in the middle of winter. Surely this silly tourist attraction, the mystery light, could not possibly be important enough for someone to put up with the desolation and miserable winter weather in this part of the country.

She knows hundreds of people who have spent days in the neighborhood trying to figure out the mystery and the source of the light but that was in the summer and fall when the wilderness is more easily accessible. Somebody is either nuts to do this in the middle of winter or something important is going on and nobody is telling little old Gail anything. She smells a very good story here. Now, she's waiting, camera in hand to photograph something.

Gail had carefully watched Arturo Smith leave the house, get into his car and turn right on the road toward Robbins Pond Road. She simply assumed that Smith was going to pay another visit to the viewing site.

At the same time, she had no idea that Robbins Pond Road had been plowed out by the county where she assumed Smith would return to take a second look at the light.

She took her usual camera package along. Telling stories was one thing. Having pictures to prove it was another matter. Gail had a thousand pictures of the light which she has taken over the years, including pictures of hundreds of tourists gawking at the light. Some she had printed in connection with human interest stories for the paper and the tourist information center because they promoted business for the area.

Gail first points the camera away from the light's usual location and toward the Robbins Pond

official viewing site. From the hill she is standing on
it's a tough chore to get a clear view. With a long lens
it's tougher still to keep the camera steady enough to
zero in on a distant photo target. After several tries
to get a clear view of the barricaded parking area, it
seems useless.

Everything is white, even the trees trunks.
Swirling and blowing snow have turned the tall
maple trees into white stems, indecipherable from the
rest of the landscape. It's a world of white, white and
more white.

Gail thought she would make out the dark
overcoat Smith was wearing when he left. It would
be interesting to have a few shots of him, their own
mystery visitor. She steadies herself against a young
maple, brings the camera to her eye and starts pan-
ning the area with the camera, by slowly moving left
to right and left again, avoiding the branches of the
elders and evergreens.

From this distance, about five hundred feet
removed from the viewing area, fir tree thickets simply will not allow her to get even a good glimpse. She
knows this area like a book. She expected that Smith,
as before, would park on the highway and walk the
snowmobile trail to the viewing site and then, from
there, attempt to continue on the snowmobile path,
where the snow is packed down, to get a closer look
at the light. That was the opportunity she was waiting for. Gail did not take into account, nor did it seem
important to her, that Smith had asked specifically
about Sleepy Hollow Road and the logging road she

took to her hill. He would not be foolish enough to attempt to reach Robbins Pond Road north of the washout section from another access road which surely would be snowed in.

These thoughts caused some frustration. *Now what?* She thought. This winter wonderland did not provide her with the opportunities she was seeking. The silence is deafening. But the woods are not silent. Not to her, they were not. This moment is no different to her then standing on her deer hunting stand during the November deer season. She had done that since she was 14 years old. There are lots of sounds in this winter wonderland that one becomes acutely aware of when knowing the north woods wilderness -- tiny brittle tree branches are cracking or breaking off from a snow load that has accumulated on them, the crunch in the snow of a small animal moving. A trained ear can pick up a snowshoe rabbit moving through the powdered snow, or breaking the crust of the snow cover. A buck can be heard moving long before one can get a good bead on him through the peep site of a 30-30 Winchester. Now, the silence and sounds of the wilderness are interrupted only by the nuisance of cars moving down the main highway, some forty acres or so away.

Maybe it's a futile effort, Gail thinks, when she turns to the sound of a crow breaking the silence. Crows are scavengers but also serve as a wilderness alert system. Very smart birds. They know everything that goes on in the woods. They would attack a rabbit or a squirrel, but sure as hell they let the Eagle know something is afoot down here. Get it while you can, so we can get what's left over. Real smart they are, Gail muses, as she watches several of them screaming away a few hundred feet up and to the north of her position. They keep the roads clean from unwanted road kill.

Gail has also done her share of wildlife photography. She's photographed eagles, their hunting skills, and the kills of their prey. She noticed many times the call of the crows alerts the eagle. When the eagle appears and soars high in the sky, the crows take a powder, until the eagle gets his prey. Then, and only then, do the crows return and take what is left. Gail is reminded of how smart and cunning these crows are. They see everything, and their timing is incredible. Crows almost never get hit by a car.

Gail has put her camera under the cover of her left armpit and looks up at the crows and then down to see a snowshoe rabbit a hundred or so feet away carelessly crossing a clearing from one clump of balsams to another.

She whips out the camera from under her arm, sets the lens on 20 millimeter, ready to zoom in. The snowshoe is under a thick balsam but what's that up above the base of the balsam and much further away in the distance? The figure of a man in a dark coat in the very middle of the woods moving from right to left. The shutter snaps once, twice and again. Then the figure disappears behind the evergreens. Gail is poised and ready for more shots. Then there is the sound of a car door slamming.

Alarmed, she turns in the direction from

whence it came, the direction of the viewing site. There are also voices heard, indecipherable but she is sure it's real. She's confused. If the figure in the woods was Smith then what's going on at the Robbins Pond Road viewing site?

She turns back to the woods, camera ready. She is cold and she knows she is not steady enough to use a long lens to get another shot of Smith. If that is who it is, she thinks.

What she now sees through the view finder is more confusing. There is a shimmer of movement in the distance where the dark figure disappeared. The figure she is observing now appears like a silver shadow moving left, then right and then away into the distance. She's not even sure it is the figure of a man. The shutter clicks again and again as fast as the manual wind will allow. She is so excited with the image, she attempts to zoom in to get a closer shot, but the camera wiggles and the silvery figure is lost to her effort, at least so it seems.

Chapter 48

At the Robbins Pond Road viewing site, one of the men belonging to the sedan with the many antennas on its roof packs up the camera gear, seemingly unsuccessful in what they attempted to do. Certainly, there was no sign of the mystery light during this daylight hours. The denseness of the forest was too thick to obtain any view similar to what Gail was able to do from the top of the hill.

One of the men is visibly upset with the failed effort and mumbles some choice words to the other, indecipherable as they are in another language. With what appears to become a gesticulated argument in a foreign tongue finally they get into the sedan and leave the viewing site, backing up toward Highway 45.

Chapter 49

Yuma Arizona

Mark Burger's offices are in a contemporary two-story, adobe-style strip mall where cars park along the entrance to the respective business offices.

It is late in the evening. A dark-colored sedan pulls into the nearly empty parking lot. Two men emerge from it. One carrying a briefcase. They head for the entrance that leads to the second floor where Burger's certified public accounting offices are located.

Mark is facing the computer screen his back toward the office entrance. He doesn't hear, or notice, the door being opened and the two men dressed in business suits who have silently entered his office. He has no chance to greet them or ask who they are. The first man has already pointed a 45-automatic with a silencer at him and fires point blank just as Mark turns to face them and before he can speak. Mark Burger sinks to the floor a thin trickle of blood runs down to the right of his nose to his mouth. Then he disappears behind his desk as his body slumps to the floor.

The two men waste no time in beginning their search for something only they, their superiors, the late Mark Burger and the Star Light Society's higher echelon directors know about. It is a two-room office with many file cabinets. Each drawer is opened, searched thoroughly and then practically pulled out of its metal roller guides and carelessly thrown to the floor.

One of the men, the assassin, a tall, slender, quite good looking man, hisses, "That's almost every file in the joint. It could be anywhere. They're a pretty clever outfit."

The other slightly shorter man, now concentrating on Burger's desk, smiles from ear to ear as he produces a large federal express envelope, yet unopened, and holds it up with a broad smile. "Will this work for us? It's from a Jason Roberts."

The first man grabs the envelope. "He could have just handed it over to us and lived. Idiot. Let's go."

The men rush out the door, leaving a tornado-like mess behind them.

Once outside, they rush to their sedan and get in, the tall man clutching the envelope under his arm. But it is too late, within a split second the car explodes sending a huge fireball toward the early evening sky.

At the end of the long hallway of the second floor where Burger's office is located, there is movement. Three men, huddled into the dark corner near the end stairwell, quickly move out of the shadows, glance into Burger's office and move down the stairs in an attempt to get out and away unseen before the authorities or a barrage of fire trucks, rescue vehicles and police cruisers arrive at the scene in the front parking lot where the destroyed vehicle is still burning.

Chapter 50

The Pentagon

Secretary Runsfeld is in a rotten mood. Everything that could go wrong, has gone wrong, and worse. Evan and Amber are sitting in front of his desk ready to be heard, ready to listen. Runsfeld turns in his high-backed swivel chair to face them. "Needless to say, I have held off your meeting with the president until we get the intelligence updates. In the meantime, Kirkland, you're lagging behind. This matter must be concluded posthaste and as efficiently as is humanly possible. You do understand that, don't you?"

Both Evan and Amber nod .

"Of course, we do," Amber answers, before Evan can. "With clarity, Mr. Secretary. But all the pieces of this very complex jigsaw puzzle are not in place yet."

Runsfeld does not like what he hears. The pressure is on him. "Like what?"He asks impatiently then pushes on. "Whatever is missing, you better find it."

"We are not sure, Mr. Secretary, if even he is able to retrieve the missing part. As we all know, we have not been able to do so for over fifty years. If, on the other hand, he is successful in doing so you can be sure we will get it," Evan says.

Evan says. "Don't be too sure. That could be a problem."He takes a file from his desk and holds it up to make a point. "Here's the bigger problem. The Bureau and the CIA reports tell us that Interpol, Russia and several international industrial conglomerates have their noses and men on the ground right under our noses." He slams the file onto his desk.

"Mr. Secretary," Amber interrupts. "If I may?"

"Go right ahead," Runsfeld comes back, a little calmer. As usual Amber's looks soften his temper.

"I have no idea, Mr. Secretary, what the specific goal of our government is, in relationship to this nonspecific thing you are talking about," Amber interjects. "I do not have the appropriate security clearance to get into that. My job was to establish a complete record of what, where and when things occurred. To maintain, not only secrecy, but, to keep the lid on, so to say."

"Mr. Secretary," Evan breaks in. "Ms. Winslow is one of the best researcher we have. She has, thus far, put the entire puzzle together, short of finding him."

Amber cuts in and manages to irritate Runsfeld a little. "And you lost him somewhere down the line. But, I am close to solving the puzzle. You think I just shuffle papers around? Not so with your superior intelligence team, like those two Idiots that just got themselves blown up, together with the vital evidence they recovered which we needed desperately." Amber pauses, hesitating for a second. "To confirm or at least come close to, the location where this physical thing you are talking about might be."

Evan tries to stop her. "Amber."

Runsfeld stares at her and cuts in. "Never mind, Kirkland, let her talk. She may be right. You can have your security clearance. Consider it done. I cannot tell you what it's all about. I cannot tell you what the urgency is and what is ultimately at stake here. Only the president himself can do that. In the meantime, I thank both of you for your efforts. Just keep it up and be ready for a briefing with the man on the hill. Whatever agency or individual help you need, you've got it."

Evan and Amber stand to leave and as they reach the door the exit is filled by an imposing, large and portly man in a tan suit, string tie and cowboy hat. He stops to admire Amber before entering.

"Excuse me," he says with exaggerated politeness in a decided Texas drawl, removing his hat and bowing slightly, stepping aside so Amber and Evan can exit.

As they walk away, they can hear his booming voice greeting Runsfeld.

"Runny ... how the hell are ya? And what's this I hear about my stock options being in trouble?"

Chapter 51

Gail is in her office, anxious to get a good look at the pictures that she took earlier in the day. She had rushed to have her 35-mm negatives developed at the Wal Mart store forty-five miles to the south of Light Struck. She only needed the negatives. She can slide them into her negative film scanning converter and print out the images from her desktop PC. With the long drive to Eagle River behind her, she proceeds with the business at hand.

She had dinner with her mom earlier, never mentioning anything about her morning venture into the woods and her attempt to find out more about Arturo Smith, and whatever he was up to. She then hurried back to the office with the negatives in her purse.

She squeezes herself into her cubby hole office, which is one thing she hates about her job. They couldn't have made it any smaller. She thinks about the idiocy of this arrangement again, unable to figure out what someone who was claustrophobic would do working in a partitioned cube less then eight-by-eight feet square. As she slides into her chair, she quickly places the negatives in the slide tray-like contraption which, like a DVD receptor, pops out a film holder and then disappears into the computer. Her fingers fly over the keyboard and, with a quick maneuver with the mouse, the first photograph appears on the computer screen.

"Shit," she exclaims loudly. "Shit." Yes, she got the picture all right, but the dark figure seen far off in the distance is not recognizable. It could be anybody in a dark coat or in a dark snowmobile suit. Certainly there is no proof that this figure is Arturo Smith. The second, the third and fourth image reveal nothing more. She is terribly disappointed but continues. Now the fifth image pops up on the screen. "Now, that's interesting," she mumbles to herself. Where the dark figure appeared on the previous photos is a faint outline of a silvery figure, nearly translucent. She magnifies the image. "Wow," The contours of a human figure can clearly be seen, resembling a figure carved out of ice or glass, except it looks so fluid, as if in motion. While it is not quite crystal clear, it has a silvery shimmer to it. She clicks on the mouse, bringing up the next image and several more. The sequential order in the style of still motion do show the different positions of the nearly translucent image, proving that it is changing positions, distancing itself from the camera location. It appears to be moving further away with each photo. This is fascinating, Gail thinks, as she pushes the print command and waits for the first of the color images to appear on the printer tray.

She could not have done any better with a digital camera, which her boss continues to urge her to use. She loves her old Nikon and Pentax 35-mm workhorses. She is a firm believer that there is nothing like film when it comes to image, sharpness, color rendition and balance.

She takes the first glossy photo from the printer tray. Fascinated with the first shot, she quickly reaches into her desk drawer to extract a large lens magnifying glass to get an even closer look at the dark figure in the wilderness. Her objective at this moment is to determine if the figure is recognizable as Arturo Smith. With anxious anticipation, she lays out the five prints neatly on her desk in sequential order. Totally engrossed in this chore she carefully examines every single print with the magnifier. Leaning down into the magnifier and the photos, it is impossible for her to notice the entrance door to the newspaper's editorial office opening silently, nor notice the shadowy figures hidden from her sight. With her preoccupation and total concentration on these most interesting and valuable photographs, she could not possibly have been aware of the silent danger that entered the deserted newspaper office. There is no way for her to notice or see the hand with an ether-soaked gauze pad that is suddenly pressed into her face with brute force.

She is helpless. After all, she was on a fact-finding mission, oblivious to anything that went on around her this evening in the empty newspaper offices where she only occasionally worked this late at night and only when trying to meet last-minute deadlines. Anything as bizarre as strangers with long coats and scarfs covering their faces mysteriously entering her workspace was just too far out to think about Everything for Gail simply fades into oblivion.

stranger quickly gathers up the photographs on her desk to follow his mate who is quickly carrying Gail off toward the exit door .

Chapter 52

Amber is planting an appreciative kiss on Evan's lips, after they enter her apartment. "Thank you, Mr. Kirkland, for voicing your appreciation of me to Runsfeld.

Evan is all smiles, having clearly enjoyed this bit of affection. She is a doll, he thinks. He never dreamed he could be so lucky, to be admired by a creature as breathtaking as Amber, of all people. After all, he is over twenty years her senior. But, forget that, he thinks. He likes it. Or is it even more then that? "You've got guts, Shatzie, and you got your A-12 clearance. Happy now?"

"I promise I won't let it go to my head." she comes back. "There is a downside to this," she adds.

"And what might that be?" Evan walks over to the armchair opposite the large couch and plops himself down.

Amber takes a seat opposite him on the couch and points to the stack of files covering the long, wide cocktail table situated between them. "We have to deliver now," she says. "And, I am not at all sure just what it is we have to accomplish?"

"It shouldn't be that complicated with what we have now. The only thing we do not know and won't know, until somebody clues us in, is what it is, this thing, that is so pivotal to this entire matter."

"And who gets to it first," Amber reminds him. Amber is wearing loose-fitting slacks and an alpaca half-length sweater which she adjusts to cover more of herself as if cold. Evan notices and suggests, "Let's address all these issues while I make a fire."

"Brilliant idea, Mr. Kirkland. It's chilly tonight. How about if we add some hot tea to the affair?"

Evan is already crumpling up old newspapers and placing some kindling wood in the fireplace. "Did you say 'affair'?" he smiles.

Amber points to the messy files on the cocktail table. "Yes, I did. I meant this mess of an affair staring us right in the face."

Evan smiles again. "Of course," he says as he puts a match to the newspaper to start the fire.

Amber moves to the breakfast counter and kitchenette, turns on the electric stove, and places a pot with water on one of the heating elements.

After adding a good-sized firewood log to the now burning kindling, he returns to the easy chair and picks up the file Runsfeld has handed over to them. He waves it in the air just to make a point. "Where do we start?"

"How about from the beginning. That way," Amber intones, "when we get called to the top, we have everything committed to memory." She adds the tea bags to the simmering water.

"Shit." Evan slams down the file. "They have everything we have. Why rehash it?

Amber lets the tea seep. "No, they do not have everything, Mr. Kirkland. We have all the gory ddetails of what happened, beginning to end. All that we need is to put this puzzle together." She pauses. "There are two issues. One, keeping the lid on. Two, how to find this thing or whatever the hell it is we yet don't know about."

Evan loves Amber's energetic and common sense approach to it all.

As she comes back to the coffee table, she uses her foot to move the files from one side to the other, making room for the teapot and cups, before he can even offer to help.

Instead, he lights up his pipe.

Amber smiles at him "Smoke away, Mr. Kirkland. I'm going to join you with a good cigarette," something he has never seen her do at the Pentagon or anywhere else for that matter. She retrieves a thin Capri cigarette from a marble cigarette box and lights it with a silver butane lighter from the adjacent end table and lights up, taking an enjoyable drag from the cigarette and looking at Evan. She is convinced now that she is in love with Evan. A real man -- mature, sophisticated and a worldly gentlemen to top it all off. *Kind, intelligent, if not brilliant. What a nice thing to have around the house.* She thinks. She is falling in love with him. Observing him closer now, she realizes her feelings are not betraying her. It's real and what she wants.

Another thing she enjoys about being with Evan is his underlying, dry sense of humor, their constant light fencing with words and innuendoes that spice up their conversations with never a dull moment, no matter how serious or secret the matter under discussion. They share so much with each other and are of like mind on so many subjects and topics. Not just limited to their work -- political beliefs and their hobbies. They are both avid readers, reclusive sometimes, at least to a degree.

Evan puffs, smoke coming from his pipe filled with aromatic Half and Half, to which he is religiously partial. He, too, is observing Amber as she thoroughly enjoys her cigarette with her tea. How could he ever be deserving of such a gorgeous creature. Why somebody has not swept her off her feet and snapped her up is just beyond him. She is the opposite of what she appears to be. She has a heart and soul and what a brain to boot, totally contradicting her outward appearance which could be taken by some as movie star or playboy centerfold, if one judged her by her figure and evenly molded facial features -- big brown eyes and fully formed luscious full lips. Not even Marilyn could upstage her, by his judgment and surely lots of other men. He watched her put her dark rimmed glasses on as she examined and sorted out some of the file folders. Now she looked like a gorgeous professor. Or was it librarian? Enough of this, he thought. How in the hell could he concentrate and think about the documents piled up high in front of him when thinking about Amber?

"Here's the poop so far," Amber breaks his thought. "New Mexico -- A UFO crashed on July 2 of 1947. Then comes the bullshit, pardon my French. Weather balloon cover-up - that worked to a degree.

The craft, what's left of it, is transported to Los Alamos first, later to Area 51 in Nevada. Before that, there were three bodies. One goes to the military hospital for autopsy, the second goes to Area 51 to be frozen. The third disappears from the local mortuary, never to be heard from again. Two witnesses. A mortician named Philip Karsten and an Army nurse named Roberson. Both dead now. Never talked. At least not that any one knows of."

"November 1947, a group called the Star Light Society comes into being in Roswell. No agency in our government ever was able to penetrate or even get close to any of its members. To this day, we don't know who they are and what they are all about. Now, in follow-up to Roswell, some twenty years later, Werner von Braun, one of our renowned German rocket scientists, formerly in the employ of Adolph Hitler, is engaged by our government to work with NASA on our space program. Von Braun introduces a friend of his Ernst Schweizer to the program."

Evan interrupts. "I don't know were this is going but I haven't come across this file before -- Ernst Schweizer? Who's he and how does he fit in?"

Amber picks up a file from the many on the cocktail table, opens it, and takes out a picture of a man resembling Arturo Smith. Age: Difficult to tell but, if one had to guess, he would be in his late thirties to mid-forties. "This, dear Evan, if you recall, this is the same gentleman that in later years we have photographs of in the McDonnell Douglas Jet Propulsion Laboratories. Later yet, the Stealth Fighter Project, but the name changed to Victor Collins. And later yet, the Star Wars program during the Reagan administration. The name then was Fred Warwick. That was the last report and the last photograph of Mr. Ernest Schweitzer, Warwick, Collins, or whatever you want to call him." Amber now spreads out three more files, opens them and places photographs of the mystery man from the files all in a row for Evan to look at. "What's so remarkable about these? He looks the same age in 1965 and in 1987. That's a 20-year span. And this, I believe, is who we are looking for at this very moment."

"In the Upper Peninsula of Michigan, no doubt," Evan says the obvious.

"And that is what Secretary Runsfeld is after, right?" Amber emphasizes. "Now we're getting a little closer to solving the puzzle," she continues. "My guess is, by the projects this guy was involved in, his whereabouts must be of some awesome importance to us."

"Right," Evan adds. "And wherever he shows up something big is going on."

Amber gives Evan her great sarcastic, antigovernment smile. "And I have a hunch that the secret to whatever it is everybody wants, just exploded into flames in Yuma, Arizona, together with two of our bureau agents."

Evan has listened carefully and soaked everything up. He was vaguely familiar with most of the events but also was aware of the fact that many files either disappeared or were simply misplaced, or mis-filed. Now, with an efficient researcher like Amber, all these highlights came into perspective again. *And they made sense, if that's at all possible,* he thought.

"By the way, who was that overstuffed Texan at Runsfeld office?" Amber asks, obviously unim-pressed.

"Don't know. Never saw him before. He just reeked of oil and bad cologne."

Evan smiles. "You don't miss a thing, do you?"

Chapter 53

It is difficult to determine the location in which the high-backed chair stands, Gail is tied to it with a rope and electrical tape. She cannot move and cannot see nor scream, her mouth strapped with tape. One dim, low wattage light bulb illuminates the bound figure, leaving everything around her in darkness. Only the faint gray outlines of a non-distinct figure behind her and one to the her right can be vaguely seen.

The shadowy figure on the right leans into her and with, a foreign accent, demands to know, "Who is this Mr. Smith?"

With this, his hand reaches for the tape covering her mouth and viciously rips it off, causing Gail to scream out in pain.

"You hear me, yes? Who is this Mr. Smith?" he repeats, angry and practically snapping his teeth into her face.

Gail moves her head sideways as much as the ropes and tape around her head permit her . "I don't know."

"We think you know. Man lives with you under roof, no?" The interrogator shows that he has no patience as he continues to question her with pure venom in his voice. "Now talk. What you know about Mr. Smith?"

"Nothing. I know nothing about him. He's just a visitor."

"You lie!" he accuses her. "But we will know soon. You will tell us little lady. You will tell us everything you know." He leans into her again and removes the scarf covering her eyes. He reaches up to the single light above her head and turns it so it illuminates her face and the immediate area surrounding her body.

Gail is petrified as she stares into the darkness, attempting to see at her captors.

"Let us show you why you will talk girl. There is much to talk with us." The man reaches behind her and is handed something by the other figure. The hand of the man is seen holding a large hypo syringe filled with a yellow liquid. He holds it up to the light at an angle so Gail can clearly see it above her.

"No problem girl, no worry, no pain, no torture, just nice talk, understand?"

Gail's eyes widen, moving wildly in search for help, but there is none. She screams. "No please no, I don't know anything. Please don't do this to me."

"Ah," says the man, "Why you then take picture of man?"

"I am a photographer and a writer, I write news."

"Good," the man says. "You know more then we think, then." Completing his sentence, he jabs the syringe into her left shoulder and pushes down on the plunger.

Gail's mouth opens wide, her eyes roll and in a beat her head slumps forward slightly before her eyes close.

Chapter 54

The only illumination comes from the three-quarter moon that casts eerie and harsh shadows from the trees onto the pristine, untouched, white snow cover of the wilderness.

Long before the figure of a being emerges from the thick spruce and balsam stands and faint sounds of footsteps are heard on the forgiving snowy surface, the slight figure of a being, human-like being no less, can be seen emerging from the thicket and crossing the clearing that gives way to the taller maple and oak trees opposite the evergreen thicket. The details of the being are obliterated it's shimmer of silver, nearly translucent.

Only upon closer observance with the help of binoculars, can one decipher that the being is indeed human in nature. Only the attire provides it with the illusion of translucency. The vision appears especially eerie when out of the shadows of the trees and exposed to direct moonlight.

The being slowly moves toward a large oak tree, grotesquely silhouetted against the ominous, partially clouded and covered sky, then to a smaller clearing adjacent to the huge gnarled oak.

In another clearing some few hundred yards away from the gnarled oak, two men are observing the ominous silvery being, moving toward the tall grotesque oak tree with high powered binoculars but even with the help of the binoculars it's impossible to definitively identify the silvery being moving with purpose through this almost idyllic moonlight wilderness setting. Nevertheless, it does resemble the figure of a man. One could have easily described the figure as a person dressed in some kind of silver lame' attire. This, of course, would be illogical in the middle of winter. Who would walk around in the woods at night with a skin tight leotards or body suit?

Strangely enough, the two men watching the mysterious figure are not at all disturbed by what they are observing, as if everything was proceeding according to plan.

The two observers seemed calm but slightly curious, watching every move being made by the enigmatic silvery figure.

Then, suddenly, there is a pencil thin beam seen coming from a gadget being held in the figure's right hand which scans the area adjacent to the oak tree. The green laser beam thoroughly covers the snowy area around the oak until it begins to emit a high pitched series of long beeps which, as the sound resolves itself, turns into a low-pitched humming sound.

The figure appears to have zeroed in on a desired source and a specific location in the ground near the oak tree and proceeds with the very same laser emitting gadget to point directly to the specific spot that caused the low humming sound to respond to the beam of light. The laser beam widens and turns red in color. Instantly, the snow melts and exposes an incredibly strange looking black round ball-like object that begins to glow, gradually emitting a greenish hue, then gradually increases intensity until the object first turns dangerously red, then into a brilliant white illuminating the entire area as if a billion foot candles had been ignited.

The entire spectacle lasts less then a few seconds, almost blinding the two observers as if a halogen spotlight had been placed inches before their eyes.

It is a spectacle to behold. The silvery figure is not only bathed in, but momentarily swallowed by it, making the light and the figure one and the same. Gradually it dims to a white greenish glow emanating from the round object lying in the snow-covered exposed hole in the earth.

The silver-clad figure bends down toward the object now and covers it with a silver cloth causing it to go totally dark. The figure's right hand reaches underneath the sphere, lifting it out of the ground and simply touches the underneath, and then removes the silver cover. There is no more light emitting from the source which is now recognizable or at least looks like a dark metal ball, the size of an ordinary basketball, maybe a little larger.

Seemingly satisfied with this accomplishment, the figure produces a perfectly square cube-like container which appears out of nowhere, then carefully places the dark ball into it, closing the lid of the container, and snaps the latches shut.   Then he picks it up by the handle and casually moves away from the site near the oak tree as if absolutely nothing out the ordinary has taken place.

The men hidden a few hundred feet in the shadows of the spruce trees return their binoculars to their leather cases slung over their shoulders and begin to move in the direction of the figure. At the edge of the woods the mysterious figure and the two men in dark winter coats meet. One of the men with a sigh of relief mutters, '"Finally it's over."

Almost in ceremonial fashion, the ominous figure nods to the men and hands them the silver cube. They accept the container and turn to leave. It is impossible, even though it is night and the light of the moon is faint, not to clearly follow the movements of the two now in possession of the silver container. Even at a distance of a few hundred yards, the ominous figure having done all the work and handed over the container, has simply disappeared.

The men in possession of the container walk through the snow in an easterly direction. Suddenly they stop, as the two figures now become four. Except that this added company is almost invisible as the figures are dressed in snow white attire, including their head covers. They too are in possession of a cube like container, similar in color and dimensions to the first. The men in white exchange containers with the two men wearing the dark overcoats. There is not a word spoken in what seems to be a well organized and well orchestrated plan to cover up what they have done.

The men in white part company and walk

north until they can no longer be seen, while the other two walk south in the direction of the Robbins Pond Road entrance to the viewing sight of the light. Anyone expecting to see two men with a container of any kind in the deep woods in the middle of the night will not be disappointed. The question, of course, will remain: Which container holds the object that was so carefully retrieved from under the snow and the earth under the gnarled old oak tree?

On Robbins Pond Road, a black SUV turns toward the viewing site of the mystery Light. One of the two men that exits from the SUV is holding a rifle in his hand as the other clutches a pair of high powered military binoculars. Silently, without even closing the car doors, they disappear into the woods.

Two hundred feet up the road to the north, a white van with multiple antennas protruding from the roof, is parked adjacent to Highway 45. Four men in camouflaged white winter military snowsuits emerge, sub machine guns in hand and scatter into the woods.

Chapter 55

The Village of Bayfield rolls up its sidewalks at dark which is just around five p.m. in the winter. At ten at night nothing moves, except for the few quaint advertising signs suspended by squeaky chains from posts or hanging over doors of the small businesses like the only grocery store, the antique shop, a gift shop and the Tourist Information Office. A strong lake breeze adds a bite to the already cold night.

A lone patrol car of the Bayfield County Sheriffs office, cruises the main thoroughfare turning down to the harbor. The Sheriff's car has just turned around at the ferry terminal and is heading back to Highway 13 and to its home-base in Washburn 10 miles down the road when a small, inconspicuous Ford Escort rounds the corner from Highway 13 to Hill Street were Jason Roberts home is located. The small blue escort does not drive all the way up to Jason Roberts' house, the intended destination, but pulls into a parking spot a block before getting to the quaint house on the hill.

Jason Roberts is dressed in a parka because it is cold topside in his observatory. He often takes advantage of clear winter nights like this to climb up to his telescope housing to gaze at the stars or just catch some unusual happening in the firmament. The drawback to this winter activity is the cold weather. The moment he opens the trapdoor to the roof of the bubble top to about 24 inches, the cold engulfs himn. It's no better then being outside.

Jason is focusing on the stars on this crystal clear night. He is oblivious to what is going on downstairs at his front door, with door opening technology foreign to him. Two men, dressed in heavy overcoats, simply apply a directional magnet on the dead bolt of his door. The steel bolt inside the brass housing of the lock reacts to this powerful technology instantly and as if there is no lock on the door at all. Without much effort or noise the men enter the house and quickly search every room for their targeted man.

Just as Jason is climbing down from his observatory by way of the retractable ladder, he feels some thing hard being forced into his back ribs. "The original negatives. Let's not waste any time." He hears the threatening voice as the pressure in his back increases.

Jason does not turn or move. He knows that whoever it is behind him means business. *What can he do?* In a sense, he has expected this type of intrusion for some time. His immediate thought is on his dead bolts. *How in the hell did someone get in?* He thought all along the extra large dead bolts should have prevent a situation like this. Damn, he thinks. What went wrong? The negatives are still on his computer desk in a manila envelope. Thank god for little favors. Copies and all other material are in his safe which may not even be an issue in this matter. "What do you want?" he mumbles making no move to turn around to face his assailant.

The intruder pushes the 45-automatice deeper into Jason's back and, with the left, hand reaches for the thick collar of his overcoat and simply jerks the rather small-framed man around in the direction of his computer room. "Your call. It's the easy way or the hard way," bellows the intruder.

With brute force, Jason is being held from the back by his coat collar, the gun in his back. He is shoved through the narrow hallway like a straw doll being lead to his study where his desk and computer are situated. It is here Jason faces another intruder, a slender man who has made a mess of his desk, the drawers and the file cabinets in the study. "I can't find a damn thing," the man shouts as Jason is being pushed into the room and is finally released.

His assailant is visible now, a tall, heavyset man in his forties. His face reminds Jason of a bulldog. "all right," he barks. "Where are they?"

Jason is not about to reason with these two, or argue. He points to a large yellow manila envelope propped up against the computer screen, untouched by the mad ravaging of his desk and drawer contents.

The bulldog shoves Jason with such force he ends up on the floor in the corner of his study. The slender man grabs the envelope, quickly opens it and extracts a handful of 35-mm negatives, proudly showing them to his partner.

Idiot," the square faced guy shouts back then, in an even louder voice, orders his partner, "Lets go," turning to leave and ignoring Jason.

"What about him?" the slender man asks.

"What about him? Let's get the hell out of here.Move!" With that, both men rush to the door the man the manila envelope in hand.

Jason is still on the floor, exhausted but relieved. Leaning on the corner wall, he pulls himself up. All he can think of is, *How in the hell did they get in?* His surefire dead bolts had failed him. Only as he hears the front door slam shut does he finally takes a deep breath of relief and collects himself. He knows what he must do -- call the Society, tell them that all is not lost. The original negs are gone but not his duplicates. Finally, as he stands, still shaky, he moves to his computer chair and he wonders, *Who were those guys?* He can only assume it was FBI or CIA.

Chapter 56

Eleanor is ascending the last tier of the steep staircase in haste. Slightly out of breath, her left hand clutches the bannister as often as necessary to reach the top floor of the three-story brick apartment building.

It is dark, except for the faint light coming from a single light fixture on the ceiling of each floor. Hallways branch out leading to apartments at each landing. Now reaching the third floor corridor, she turns left then stops and knocks on the door closest to her on her right. She waits impatiently for someone to answer. First, there is noise coming from the inside as the peephole shutter clicks. She knows she can be seen by her friend Grace. Then, the door opens wide as an elderly woman with dark hair covered with a badly and unevenly tied babushka tied around it greets her.

"Eleanor, what a surprise. Come in, come in." With that she steps aside as Eleanor enters.

The living room of the apartment into which Eleanor steps is as dimly lit as the stairway and the halls of the building. The dark brown and black furniture make the surroundings feel even more depressing. The many decorative items with fringes do little to cheer up the room. Every table is covered with table clothes with long dark colored fringes. The old lamps with their hundred year old lamp shades have fringes hanging from their edges to further block the light from the lowest wattage bulbs available.

"Sorry to barge in like this, Grace," Eleanor says with a tone of apology, still standing in the middle of the living room.

"Don't worry, dear, sit down please." She pauses. "Or should we go right into the den?" Grace points to a doorway to another room that is separated by a full-beaded curtain, covering the entire doorway.

"You look wonderful, Eleanor." Grace smiles. "Need some tea, or maybe a glass of wine? You have something on your mind that needs talking about. Come on, I'll get you a glass of wine, and then we can talk."

Knowing well Grace will not take no for an answer, she follows Grace into the den through the beaded curtains that lead into an even darker area than the halls and living room. The den is a ten-by-ten foot room without visible walls because they are covered completely with dark red curtains. The only furniture is in the middle of the room a round table with two chairs opposite one another. A large illuminated crystal ball adorning the center of the table provides the only light.

Eleanor has been here before and simply sits were she always sits, her back to the beaded door leaving the chair opposite her for Grace to occupy.

Grace has rushed out and is now returning with a small silver tray with two glasses and a bottle of Mogan David wine. She pours no more then an ounce or so into the glasses and sinks into her chair, her dark brown eyes illuminated slightly by the shimmer of light from the crystal ball provides all the characteristics of a gypsy fortune teller. Grace is just that -- a medium and psychic.

Grace takes a sip of wine. "What's up my dear. Something is bothering you." Not waiting for an answer, she continues. "It is not negative energies this time, I think we took care of those the last time you were here." Grace runs her hand over the crystal ball and the colors change from amber to a light green and are actually more soothing and comforting, Eleanor thinks.

"We took care of your uncle and grandfather last time you were here and I know they have not returned to the lodge. You are confused about something, a man, I can feel it." Her hand moves again over the crystal ball and the color changes to a pinkish red.

"You are right, Grace. I am confused." Eleanor takes a sip from her glass. "I need to ask you a simple question."

"Something about a man." Grace states with conviction.

"Yes and no," Eleanor says. "Nothing complicated I hope."

"I can feel something but, as you know, I cannot read minds so tell me?"

"Grace," Eleanor begins. "Tell me, does everyone have an aura?"

"Of coursse." Grace comes back. "I can see yours now -- wonderful -- nice color and very strong, and radiant."

"But does everyone have one?" and she intones, "everyone."

"All living things have an aura. Some less detectable than others."

Eleanor is anxious. "What if one cannot detect or see it?"

"Then there is something wrong with you as an observer or the subject you are attempting to focus on. I happen to know, you're pretty good at that. So what is the problem?"

Eleanor empties her glass of wine. "We have a house guest. Just the nicest gentleman you'll ever want to meet but, no matter what I did and how hard I've tried, I cannot detect an aura."

"Interesting." Grace smiles, but seems unconcerned. "So, tell me about this gentleman." She moves her hand over the crystal ball and it glows dark red now. "I feel two things, give me one moment of silence." Grace closes her eyes for several seconds. "I feel something, but see nothing. There are matters you are not talking about and refuse to talk about. Whatever the reason may be, it's blocking your abilities to see. But, there is something else. Your subject, your guest, what is his name?"

"Arturo, Arturo Smith."

Again, Grace closes her eyes for a moment. "I see an aura, of a kind I have never observed before, huge, full of color." Grace closes her eyes again as if enjoying every second of what she is experiencing. "Absolutely beautiful." She continues with her eyes closed. "Not of this world. When can I meet this gentleman?"

"I don't know. I don't know how long he will be staying, but what is wrong with me then, why can I not detect his aura?'

"Because," Grace opens her eyes. "Because you are withholding something. You're abilities are impaired. It's called blockage. Now I feel some negative energies, but they do not come from those gone. These are dark energies from live entities. If that helps you any."

Eleanor slowly gets up from the chair. "Well, I will just have to work that out. It's a long drive and I better be going."

"You'll be just fine Eleanor." Grace gets up to see her friend out.

Chapter 57

Arturo Smith enters the Bed and Breakfast, ready to move up the stairs that lead to the second floor from the hallway entrance. He stops cold when he hears a voice from the area of the living room -- Gail's voice.

Gail is lying on the couch, her eyes closed, her face badly bruised. Her head moves violently side to side. She attempts to scream out loud but cannot get her voice to cooperate. Only low-volume whispers escape her mouth. "No more. Please, no more."

Smith enters the living room and kneels down next to her.

Gail continues to repeat the same words over and over again. Traumatically moving her head from side to side. "No more, please no more."

Smith holds his hand over her forehead but does not touch her. Still dressed in his overcoat he reaches into his pocket to extract a small gadget, triangular in shape, and no larger then the palm of his hand. The glassy underside of the triangle emits rays of light accompanied with a low intermittent humming sound. After he holds and moves the triangular object over Gail's body in a scanning fashion, her forced whispers become clear sounding words.

"I don't know. Please, no more."

Smith holds the triangle over her forehead for a prolonged time until a calming effect can be seen in Gail's features. Smith manipulates the triangular gadget for a second, then scans her entire body with it. Gradually, to his satisfaction, he can see the bruises on her face disappear and Gail seems to be resting comfortably.

Smith places the triangle back into his coat pocket then places his fore and middle finger on the left temple of Gail's head. She remains calm, undisturbed. Smith is satisfied, then quickly moves toward the winding staircase in the living room and energetically ascends to the second floor.

Chapter 58

The sounds of a wailing siren are coming from the sedan with an overabundance of red and blue flashing strobe lights mounted on its dashboard and the rear window of the black sedan as it speeds toward the Pentagon. Traffic is brisk and causes numerous unwanted obstructions.

But this is an urgent matter, a few scrapes here and there, scaring the daylights out of pedestrians and innocent bystanders, does not count. It does however, cause concern to Washington's Police Department and the regular police squad cars which have not a clue of what is going on, and simply follow the speeding, screaming vehicle. They have not been alerted to anything from within the department or from sources higher up.

The only action to take is to follow the leader, just in case some help is needed at whatever destination they are speeding to. On the other hand, if it turns out not to be an official, authorized vehicle, the Police Department squads would simply close in and overwhelm the perpetrators.

Some of the squads have radioed in and are still trying to establish some communications with their headquarters, the Bureau and even CIA headquarters, but it is either "we don't know," or no answers period. Only after 20 police squads are tailing the sedan, does the destination of the speeding, wailing and flashing, black sedan become obvious, as it is heading right for the Pentagon and the private tunnel entrance to which there is access only for high ranking officials and class A-12 security cleared individuals. The police squads, all 20 or more of them, come to a screeching halt at the entranceway. They know just too well nobody gets in unless it's big brass or some big stuff is going on.

Chapter 59

Inside the Pentagon two men, one carrying a large manila envelope, rush to an underground facility marked in small inconspicuous letters, "Laboratory." It is a computer-filled photographic examination facility were all photographic intelligence images are gathered, examined and thoroughly analyzed, be they satellite images, spy plane transmissions or internet imaging intelligence, or something as antiquated and out dated as 35-millimeter film

It's a digital high-definition world. Most of the highly qualified personnel manning this department, while intrigued with old technology, are simply not used to working with it.

When the large manila envelope is handed to the white haired elderly gentleman, Jim Mahoney, head of the department, he simply asks the two men having delivered the packet to him, "When do they want it?"

"Yesterday or before," is the response from one of the men.

Mahoney opens the envelope and extracts a handful of a wildly assembled 35-mm film negatives.

The men watch him, then turn to leave. "It's all yours," one of them mumbles before they depart.

Chapter 60

Eleanor enters her living room and finds Gail sleeping on the couch. She expected her daughter to be at work. It's late in the afternoon, already. Eleanor quietly leans over Gail and touches her shoulder gently. "Gail."

Gail moves slightly but does not answer or open her eyes. Eleanor is concerned and she tries again.

"Gail, darling, are you all right?' Her hand gently shakes Gail's shoulder. "Taking a nap at this hour, what's wrong?"

Now, Gail begins to wake, drowsily she opens her eyes. At first she does not see her mother, who moves back to take a seat on the edge of the couch. Only after staring at the ceiling and an attempt to recognize her familiar surroundings, does she move her head and look at her mother. "What time is it?"

Eleanor looks at her watch, "Almost five o'clock."

Gail is confused, realizing, however, that she is in the safety of her own living room and in the presence of her mother, representing a calming effect. "You must be kidding. I was going to work late tonight but I felt sleepy and just wiped out."

"Where is Mr. Smith?" Eleanor inquires out of curiosity.

"No clue, Mother," she says. "I am supposed

to be at work. Something strange happened to me, but I don't know what it is." She moves her body slightly upward in an attempt to get up, but her head feels like a lead ball on her shoulders. "Where is my briefcase, Mother? Would you get it for me?"

Eleanor stands and begins to search around the living room area, then moves into the dining and kitchen area. She cannot locate it. "Sorry dear, it's not around here anywhere. What's so important about your briefcase?"

"I never go anywhere without it. I must have left it at the office." Gail makes another move to sit up but allows her body to sink right back into the couch instead.

"You're not all right, are you?"

"I am fine Mother, just had a terrible night-mare, way out kind of stuff, that's all. That's why I have to get to the office and get my briefcase. My wallet is in there."

"I just don't understand darling but if that's what you have to do so be it."

Gail makes another attempt to sit up. There is an improvement but her head still feels heavier then it should. "Yeah well, where is Mr. Smith? I could swear he was here just awhile ago." Gail gets to her feet, sways a moment then grabs her overcoat. "I won't be long mother, and I'll be just fine," she adds, seeing her mothers concerned look.

"All right, darling, please drive carefully and when you get back I must talk to you about something very important.

Now it's Gail's turn to be confused. She hides her feelings but she knows something is not quite right. Her head hurts and her recall of anything that has happened to her in the past 20 hours is a total zero. The last thing she can remember is working on her computer, scanning in negatives and printing some pictures. There it all stops, except for an image of Arturo Smith leaning over her looking at her and comforting her. She recalls an easing of the pain she had experienced when seeing Smith, plus a feeling of complete trust and comfort. Then, she must have fallen asleep.

Chapter 61

Ten minutes later she enters her office and turns on the computer. Waiting for the old Mac to boot up, she looks around for her briefcase. It is exactly in the spot where she had put it the night before -- on top of the computer hard drive. "But was it the night before? Or maybe the night before that?" She is angry with herself for not being able to clearly remember just what is what. Stubborn as she is, she turns her attention toward the computer and brings up the files she remembers posting on the desktop. The icon was titled "Woods Pics". She positions the cursor on the desktop item and clicks on it. The screen is filled with the wording file deleted.

"Damned son of a bitch." She swears to herself. This is too much to take. What happened? Desperately, she tries to remember. Her mind just draws a blank. She paces the floor outside her little cubbyhole office, briefcase in hand, then stops to open the briefcase. Everything is in order the way she recalls it. Her wallet is inside the case seemingly untouched. Her angry pacing is interrupted by the ring of the telephone in her office.

"Gail here," she answers it.

The voice on the other end is Cheryl's

"What's up on your end?" Gail asks impatiently.

"Well, I got something for you," Cheryl

replies, "But you may not like what you're going to hear."

"Yeah, why? I've got problems of my own," she says out loud. "But, what's up anyway?"

"Search your memory," Cheryl commands. "Who prompted you to get involved with the Star Light Society and attend all the meetings? Search your soul girl. You'll remember."

"Right now, I'm not too good at remembering much of anything. Why is that important?"

"Think, please. It is important," Cheryl persistently tells her.

"You did, if I remember correctly. Sure, it was you, Cheryl."

"Wrong," Cheryl comes back. "It was not me, it was your mother, Gail. And cutting through all the crap, the answer to everything you are seeking is right under your nose at home," Cheryl intones. "With your mother."

Gail is confused and her anger grows. "You must be mad. What's wrong with you, Cheryl? And why can't you tell me what's going on?"

"Way too complicated. But, I promise you, Gail, you have nothing to worry about that house guest of yours, Mr. Smith. He's a friend, a real friend to all of us. Just ask your Mom about him and the Star Light Society. And one more thing, whatever was going on, or coming down, if that's the way you want to put it, it's nearly over, for the most part, it's done."

"What are you talking about," Gail practically

screams into the phone.

There is a slight click and the line goes dead.

Gail had left the house with a slight headache, but calm. Now, she storms out of the office, upset, confused, and very angry.

Chapter 62

"Mother! Mother!" Gail hollers as she enters the Bed & Breakfast Lodge and storms into the living room.

"In the kitchen, dear," comes the reply from Eleanor.

Gail storms into the kitchen. She is furious.

"Mother, we need to talk."

"Yes, dear. What's troubling you?"

"Where is Mr. Smith?"

"I don't know if he is upstairs or out," Eleanor says calmly as she lights a cigarette.

"All right, then let me ask you this. Who is Mr. Smith?"

Her mother remains calm. "How should I know? You know as much as I do."

Gail sits down opposite her mother at the kitchen table and looks at her. "I don't think so. Remember when you coaxed and pushed me to join the Star Light Society? The meetings, you thought, would be a nice way for me to make friends. You always said I would meet nice people."

"You did enjoy going. And you did make friends. What was wrong with that?"

"Mother," Gail pushes. "How come you knew so much about them and were so pushy? You're hiding something."

Eleanor puts the cigarette out, grinding the

butt into the ashtray and immediately lights another one, then looks straight at her daughter.

"Oh my, you do know, don't you?" She pauses. "But, dear, there was no reason for me to tell you that I was part of them and still am. Is that what's bothering you?"

"It is," Gail shoots back. "And what about Mr. Smith. Is he here by sheer coincidence or is there more to it?"

"Dear, you know what the Star Light Society is all about. When they get confirmation of a real event or encounter, they are there to help. And if good ole Uncle Sam tries to cover something up, we try our best to uncover it."

"I kind of sensed or knew that. What does this have to do with Mr. Smith, Mother?'

"Remember when we watched that television show, 'Unsolved Mysteries' featuring the Roswell incident?"

"Yes, Mother, I remember it well. We watched it at least three times since then."

"Well good," Eleanor continues. "Then you'll remember the part about the nurse that was the eye-witness to it all."

"What are you talking about?" Gail interrupts.

"The alien autopsy, of course, and the mystery of the one who survived."

"I remember that all too well. What's the point?"

"The nurse, my dear daughter, was your

grandmother, my mother."

"Oh, my God." Gail is shocked and speechless for a few seconds. "Mother, you are putting me on."

"I'm afraid not. All the facts are in a document case in my bedroom upstairs, including your grandmother's diary."

Gail stands up and paces the floor, overwhelmed with what she has just been told. "Cheryl was right," she mumbles. "What has all that to do with Mr. Smith?"

"You may want to sit down for this one," Eleanor suggests. "Our Mr. Smith is the one survivor of that crash."

The normal color leaves Gail's face as she gasps and sits down. She has been through a lot as an amateur UFOlogist, and as a writer and reader of science fiction. She has given a lot of thought about the world, the universe, what it could be like to have an actual encounter with an extraterrestrial. This is different though. Altogether different. Way too close to home, too bizarre and difficult to accept, at least for the moment.

"Are you telling me Mom, that he's an alien? An extraterrestrial?

Eleanor helps her along. "Helped by the Society to fulfill a most important mission on this planet."

Gail stands again. She has to do something to help her digest it all. She paces the kitchen floor. "First, Mother, I have to get used to this science fiction reality. If you want to call it that. Then I have to cope with a million questions that come to mind. And that's not all. Then I have to ask, now what?"

Chapter 63

Even though it is late at night at the Pentagon Photo Research Laboratory, it is as busy as ever. The positive 35-mm film images, taken by Jason and retrieved by two CIA operatives who delivered them to Washington, are now being enlarged to two-foot-by-two-foot transparencies hanging on a back lit glass screen. Mahoney, laser pointer in hand, explains his findings to Evan and Amber. The fine red laser zeros in on one of many UFOs clearly seen in a night sky.

"Frame One,"Mahoney explains. "UFO enters frame according to all calculations, from over Toronto, Canada, near the northeastern part of Lake Ontario. Date: July 2, 1947. Time: 4:33 a.m. Good rendition and enough detail, as you can see, to determine the exact contours of the craft. Frame Two: Basically the same image, same contours, please notice the protrusion on the top and the one underneath the craft. There are two protrusions, a large one and one a little smaller in size, measured in circumference and height." The laser dot rests on the underneath of the UFO where a small half-sphere form can be seen.

Evan and Amber are watching intently.

"Frame number three,"Mahoney moves his laser dot to the little white sparkles appearing underneath the craft. "What are these?"   He asks turning to Evan. Because there is no reply, he continues. "Something happened to that craft. A malfunction of some kind and the likely cause of the Roswell crash moments later. The proof is here now. Frame numbers four, five, and six. There is something missing from underneath the craft."

The laser dot now moves to the transparencies indicated. What was seen in frame one and two are no longer part of the craft after the sparks appeared as shown in frame number three.

"This is the other missing link," Amber blurts out. "So, what happened to that missing part? I don't suppose you could ever figure that out?"

"Maybe not with a one hundred percent certainty, but I would bet we could rely on 99 percent and leave one percent to theory." Mahoney now positions the laser dot on an enlarged image of frame number five. The naked eye can barely make out the image resembling dust spots against the black sky. "Whatever this is, it descended vertically and rapidly, directly over the Upper Peninsula of Michigan. Either it disintegrated before reaching earth, or it did on impact." Mahoney turns to Amber and Evan. "As you know all reports point to the fact that something crashed to the ground on that specific night, at that specific time, in the vicinity of Bruce Crossing, Michigan."

The laser dot zeros in on yet one other photo. The image is black except for a series of intermittent vertical dots, coming from nowhere in the sky and descending to earth. "This is the very best we can do to confirm that something left that space craft and crashed to earth moments before the craft reached the desert near Roswell, crashing as well." Mahoney puts the laser pointer down.

Amber has one question she must ask. "What is it that separated from that ship?"

"That Amber, you have to ask you know who." He gives her a thumbs up.

"Nevertheless, it's only an opinion. Could well have had something to do with whatever makes those things fly at light speed. Some malfunction. Seems like something came off of that craft and caused it to crash."

Chapter 64

The Secretary of Defense, Ed Runsfeld, pushes the button on his speaker phone, puffing on his genuine Havana cigar, a gift from a CIA operative who was lucky enough to get away alive with a few boxes of Castro's personal inventory while on a mission which had failed miserably -- another attempt to do away with Fidel just a few months ago.

The voice on the speaker identifies itself as, "Evan Kirkland, Mr. Secretary. The Society has received the goods. Everything went wrong Mr. Secretary. The goods were being tracked by several agencies as you know. There was a shoot-out. Agent Kelly was killed, but most of the Interpol and KGB guys are history."

"That's a comfort," Runsfeld barks into the speaker with sarcasm. "But the Society got the goods. What about him?"

"We think we know where to find him. What do you want us to do?"

"Never mind about him. We better know where that damn thing is or where it is going and how to retrieve it. Sons of bitches they are."

"One word of comfort sir," Kirkland's voice comes back. "It's in our country somewhere and it didn't get into the wrong hands. As you said, sir, that was critical."

"Never mind that right now. Get on those

bastards and get what we're after. No mistakes, no excuses."He slams his finger on the speaker button, ending the conversation. He is livid, unable to maintain control of himself as he violently pushes the burning tip of the cigar into a stack of papers on his desk which begin to smolder. Realizing this irrational move, he's now compelled to busy himself putting out the smoldering documents. "Rotten SOBs."

Runsfeld turns to the visitor sitting in his office, holding the ten-gallon hat on his lap.

"There better be no more screw-ups," the man says, "or the campaign chest will be pretty empty next time around."

Chapter 65

Eleanor, Gail and Arturo Smith are gathered in the living room of the Bed and Breakfast Lodge.

Smith looks at Gail and in a soft kind voice, says, "I am happy, Miss Gail, that you understand and can accept the facts as they are." His body language expresses satisfaction as he folds his hands over his knees.

"I am not at all sure I do understand. As far as accepting the facts as they are, I am not so sure. You tell me, Mr. Smith, I should be capable of understanding all of this, including your presence here. I'm very mixed up. A common weakness of us here on earth. After all, I've never experienced anything like this, if you know what I mean?"

"Miss Gail," Smith replies. "I have become quite accustomed to dealing with human emotions and traits. I can say with conviction that you are quite an extraordinary human being, very much like your mother and your grandmother."

"Thank you," Gail answers. "That's quite a compliment. I still have a lot of questions."

"We have only a limited amount of time, Miss Gail. First of all, it would be useless for me to even attempt to explain my being as it appears to you at this very second and in your time frame. But, as the earth and all life on it evolves, the secrets of reality, physical mass and caliptical perception, will become a matter of common acceptance.   Please, do not attempt to understand everything now. It would compare to an attempt to persuade cavemen to understand jet propulsion or anything of the primitive technology used today in your daily lives, which you refer to as high-tech."

Eleanor is listening intently, mouth agape. Much of what Smith has said is going over her head.

Gail quickly admits, "I can accept the fact that I can't understand what is simply beyond me. What I will understand, however, if you could tell me, why this visit to us to this area is so important? In plain English, why are we here now? Together? What's it all about?"

"That I can tell you now," Smith begins. "You see, Miss Gail, the Roswell incident, as it is commonly referred too, was real. The space ship in question developed some difficulties and lost its power supply. This energy source landed here in this area, Miss Gail, and it had to be retrieved at all costs."

"Why?" Gail shoots back quickly.

"Because it is an incredible source of everlasting energy that could change life on Earth forever. For that matter, for all living things in the universe. All of your primitive energy resources will soon be depleted. New innovative discoveries of energy such as your nuclear development will be destructive beyond your comprehension, soon. What has been just recovered now and given to your Star Light Society, can change everything."

"Why the Starlight Society? Why us?" Gail's inquisitive and inquiring mind keeps working.

"Because from the day of the accidental arrival at Roswell, your government has indeed made sure the truth would have to be withheld from the masses. But, your Star Light Society came into being, incidentally created and organized by names you will recognize -- Hought, Brazel, Jopice, Blanchard, not to mention your grandmother. Hundreds of others joined, devoted to the truth. Sheltering and protecting me was another Society mission of the society. It is the Society, that will see to it that the energy source is not misused as it would be by yours or other governments for political purposes, or by conglomerates who wish to maintain and control the financial powers they have. I assure you, if the source falls into the wrong hands, life on your planet would change drastically. Besides, the energy it represents, it also represents power."

"Oh my god, I just thought of something. If that is what you removed, it was also the source of the light. What happens to our Mystery Light of the UP? Our tourist attraction?"

"Not to worry." Smith replies. "If your United States Forest Service claims that the light comes from a ghost, the ghost will remain, I am sure."

Chapter 66

One of the most desolate and remote areas in the country is the the northwestern Upper Peninsula of Michigan where copper mining history goes back to the age before the great pyramids of Egypt were built, when ancient civilizations toiled with the most primitive of tools to extract the red gold from under the crust of the earth. It is a geographical area that, in all likelihood, held the largest copper deposits in the world.

The Star Light Society has, for good reason, chosen this specific area as one of its preferred operating centers and is now determined to use the assets and resources of this historic and rugged wilderness area as the secure hiding place for the energy source Arturo Smith has now retrieved for them. Only the Star Light Society and its devoted members have done extensive research surrounding the many mysteries of the Upper Peninsula of Michigan. Only they, and a select group of it's members, know that a solid granite mountain has been cut into with laser like instruments and precision some five thousand years ago when humans were just learning to master bronze. Yet the precision laser like cuts in the solid granite are there for man to see, if one knows where to look.

Much research has gone into the electrical currents that permeate and emanate from huge copper formations still located under the earth in the North-

Northwestern UP, commonly referred to as stray volt-
age, or step current. It is now the Society's theory
that this very current generated by these huge copper
deposits could well be responsible for the malfunction
of the craft before it crashed at Roswell.

The swell and surge of energy at that particular
split second in time, when the craft entered the space
directly over the Upper Peninsula and, more specifically, the area of Mass City and White Pine, known to
hold large underground copper deposits, disrupted
the power source of the UFO and caused the malfunction.

Chapter 67

Almost immediately after Mahoney, in the photo research lab, had clued Evan and Amber in on the photographic evident, Amber had gone to work to do some serious research on the Upper Peninsula of Michigan. Simple reasoning told her that, in the entire history of UFO research, there had never been any confirmed evidence of a malfunction of an extraterrestrial flying object. There was the incident in Siberia, but that time the Soviets would not share anything with the West, yet alone the United States.

She was convinced, after studying the photographic evidence, that something extraordinary caused this specific malfunction and the crash to happen.

Now that she was deep into her research regarding this fascinating copper mining area and its history, she was becoming more convinced by the second that this particular geographical area may well have had something to do with what went on in space that fateful night. Yet, at the same time, something else occurred to her.

She recalled a moment in time, when she first met Evan, and the matter of locating the mystery man came up, Evan kept asking again and again, "Why would anyone want to go to the desolated areas of the Upper Peninsula of Michigan." That's what got her started. Then it became an obsession. A good question. And, it deserved an answer.

Talking with Evan about this, for the first time in their relationship, got her no where. Evan was under heavy pressure from the secretary and these latest reports were not very encouraging. On the contrary, what happened was a another major blunder by the Bureau. So they eliminated the competition by getting one of their own killed but what they were really after simply got away. Disappeared into thin air. "The goods," as this thing was called, ended up in the hands of the Star Light Society.

After the meeting with Runsfeld, Evan and Amber finally knew all the players and had a glimpse of the playing field.

Evan enters the office and sees Amber still working on piles of papers, but at this moment simply does not care. He had three meetings with the secretary and one short one at the oval office under his belt, now to preoccupy his mind.

"You look awful," Amber said to him. "How about cooling it for a while so I can give you some more information?"

He almost snaps back at her, but waves her off while he plops into the first chair he can reach, then proceeds to light his pipe. "Spare me. Anything added to this mess is unimportant, sorry."

"I don't think so," she snaps back, slightly annoyed.

"I do," he says, standing firm. "Two things are important now. Nothing else counts. One: the retrieval of the energy source and, two: finding our mystery man. Mr. Smith. How, what, why and where are all bullshit. It doesn't matter."

"Energy source? I haven't heard that before, that's what was referred to as 'the goods'?"

"A source so valuable and far reaching it would solve all energy problems on earth. And the United States must be in possession and total control of it. That's what the man in the oval office demands. Everything else, Shatzie, you can put in a final report which, knowing you, will include everything and volumes of it."

"This energy source ... What else can you tell me about it?"

"Why in the hell do you want to know?" He is exhausted as he snaps back at her.

She attempts to explain her motive. "Now that you mentioned this to me it all fits -- geographically, copper, electrical currents, energy."

"I still don't know of what the hell you're talking about. In the meantime, however, I would suggest we pack some clothes and take a trip to you know where and get a little closer to the action."

Chapter 68

In the dark of the night, the Adventure Mine near Mass City, Michigan, is buzzing with activity. The Adventure has seen better times a hundred or so years ago when it was an operating, deep shaft copper mine. Today it is a remnant of the past and occasionally during the summer months opens its doors to tourists and visitors to the Upper Peninsula who wish to explore the cold dark caves of the mine in search of copper and sometimes silver samples. These minerals are still very evident in the depths and crevices of the mine's remaining horizontal shaft. The vertical shaft that descends over 1,500 feet into the earth is blocked off to all visitors except Adventure Mine personnel, less then a dozen people.

It is exactly this vertical shaft which will temporarily become the hiding place of the cube-like container which holds the alien energy source. While a dozen or more men equipped with lanterns and flashlights are busy lowering the encased energy source into the vertical shaft of the mine there is a high-level executive meeting taking place in the basement of the retail store and home of the Adventure Mine owner.

A computer e-mail message is being prepared by one of the Star Light executives. This is to be sent to three other e-mail addresses in far away places across the United States and then finally will be forwarded to the Secretary of Defense and to the President.

The message reads:

Dear Mr. President,

As you well know, the Star Light Society is in possession of something the government not only wants but desperately needs. We wish to do what is best for America. We shall be happy to turn over the energy source to you immediately upon your inform- ing every media source that the Roswell Incident was real but covered up by the government. Once you release the truth and admit to the cover-up, the energy source is yours. Please do not procrastinate as other countries and certain conglomerates are more than willing to pay a high price for what we have. The government confession must include the facts of the extraterrestrials, the autopsy and the survivor.

Once every media source carries the truth and your admission of the cover-up, the energy source will be delivered to you forthwith.

Your friends,

The Starlight Society

Seconds after the message is composed it is sent via e-mail and into the ether.

Chapter 69

First the communication rooms of the White House and at the FBI go ballistic in its attempts to determine the message's origination point. In a conference room near the Oval Office, a dozen or so high echelon officials assemble. Heads of the CIA and the Bureau, Defense Department Chief Runsfeld, Vice President Schenley several four-star generals and an assortment of senators and representatives.

The president is silently leaning back in his chair staring at the ceiling in an attempt to maintain his composure and restrain himself. Besides Iraq, this is another powder keg that has been place at his feet with the fuse burning. How in the hell was he going to explain a fifty-plus-year cover-up by the government. On the inside he was boiling. The silence in the room is deafening. Everyone is waiting for the chief executive to say the first word.

Finally, he leans forward folding his hands on top of his desk and nods. "This is blackmail, and, we haven't a clue of how to even find them, let alone stop them. I want suggestions, intelligent ones."

"Mr. President," the Secretary of Defense starts. "We cannot possibly give in to these bastards and tell the world we lied."

"But we did," comes the word from Senator Zucker, a member of the Senate Foreign Relations Committee.

"They're not going to pin this one on me," the President snaps back unexpectedly.

"It was Truman and Eisenhower who should take the brunt of this." The Vice President interjects. "And every President thereafter. We can't let this become a partisan issue, Mr. President. It's a government issue."

"One that could sink the government. Do you know what that means gentlemen? All credibility goes down the pipe, the little that is left and that's not much," the President concludes.

"Mr. President," General Burns leans forward to look directly at his commander-in-chief. A special forces strike. Do away with every member of that militia thug operation. I think we could arrange that."

"And just where would you begin?" asks Senator Zucker. "Army Rangers parachuting onto a bed and breakfast?"

General Burns looks at the head of the CIA and the head of the Bureau but they do not react.

"Surely, we must have some intelligence on their whereabouts to get a bead on them?"

"Unfortunately not." remarks the head of the Bureau. "They are not criminals and they are not on any suspected terror list."

"That never stopped you before." Mutters Burns.

Irritated, the president stops this from going any further. "How much time do we have?" he asks

"Tomorrow morning, 11 o'clock," Runsfeld

says.

Senator Stuart, a short slender man with large horned rimmed glasses, asks to speak. "Mr. President, may I make a suggestion?"

"Go ahead, George."

"It seems to me, sir, this matter goes back fifty-plus years. Like you said, how could anyone blame us. Or you? We didn't cover anything up. Things were different then. Cold war policies put a different spin on the story."

Sam Broker, new chief of the Bureau cuts in. "Forget it. "That Star Light bunch are too smart for that. They are not just a group of sci-fi freaks, not some damn UFO nuts waiting to hitch a ride to another planet. They claim UFOs are real."

Runsfeld smiles at Broker. "Ironic you should put it that way, since they, and we, all know that they are real indeed."

"That's why we are all sitting here on a hot seat," Senator Zucker concludes.

Senator Stuart adjusts his huge, glasses pushing them up to the bridge of his nose, and hesitantly speaks up again. "We can tell em about the flying disc, the UFO I mean. But we cannot possibly say anything about the." He hesitates, then almost whispers, "The Alien."

"Good point, Senator," replies Bill Saunders, CIA Chief. "No aliens. Everybody in the world will be expecting us to show them a little green man if we admit anything about an alien."

Senator Stuart propels his tiny frame out of

his chair. "Excellent idea, better yer, spread the wordabout a new energy source for America and anything as UFOs will pale in comparison. After all, Mr. President, people are more concerned with the price of gas than they are with a flying saucer having landed somewhere over fifty years ago."

"What about the man?" asks the President, "Whatever name he's been going under, Collins, Smith, Schweizer, Williams, or whatever. He's safe and out of the way without a chance of something surfacing later?"

"It's safe to say he is still our man," Runsfeld assures everyone.

"Then why in the hell didn't he hand the goods over to us when he recovered them?" booms the voice of the CIA Chief.

"Because, for sixty years, its the society that protected him when we could not." Runsfeld replies. "I can say with certainty our man is being taken care of and the matter is under control."

A portly man, sitting in corner listening to the conversation, stirs. "You let it get out of hand, Runny," the Texan speaks up. "there is another way."

"What have you got in mind, JR?" the President asks.

"A little western subterfuge. We let these Star Light folks think they've won. Make it seem like we're putting out the word to the world and everyone. Then, when we've got this here energy supply in hand, we can do whatever we want with it -- use it or hide it real good."

The President turns to the head of NSA. "Can we do that?"

"We'd need the help of the media, but that's another can of worms."

Chapter 70

In the Bed & Breakfast kitchen, Gail and Smith are sitting opposite each other at the table.

"Mr. Smith, Arturo, I mean, so you knew my grandmother? What was she like? I was a baby when she died. I don't remember her very well."

"A very kind and intelligent human being. Much like yourself."

Gail blushes slightly. "What happens now? The Society has the energy source. What will they do with it now?"

"One way or another, your government will be the recipient and I hope they will know how to use it wisely and appropriately for the good of all. I owe a great debt to the Society. The crystal source had to go to them first, then to your leaders. There are reasons for that."

"Is it safe now?"

"Better than anywhere else on earth. There is much wrong with your government, but it is by far the safest and best place for it compared to other regions and their leaders. Maybe from here it will spread democracy, as you call it, and do away with these measures of war and armed conflicts." Smith pauses doubtfully, shaking his head. "A tall order as you would say but there is always hope and one more thing you can pass on to the others in the Society. Much effort, research and scientific experiments will be required to use the crystal properly and make it work for the good of the entire planet."

"What happens now. Where will you go and what will you do?"

Smith looks at the ceiling and, with a faint smile, says, "Oh, I don't know, but I have been in this uniform much too long and it has been a journey actually never planned. It just happened."

Chapter 71

The headlines of the Michigan Globe the next morning read:

Roswell UFO crash real.
US Government disclose
Administration admits to massive cover-up.

Both the Associated Press and Reuters have spread the headlines around the world.

Chapter 72

BERLIN,GERMANY

Chancellor Merkel is heading toward the Bundestag building where she will be shown the model of the new Bundesnachrichtendienst, (BND,) the new $920-million intelligence headquarters in Berlin to be completed by 2012. It is the largest state sponsored new construction project since World War II. When completed, the massive intelligence complex will house over 4,000 intelligence employees.

The chancellor's predecessor, G. Shroeder, argued that when flash-point situations arise in the world and the lives of German citizens are endangered, the government has to react and be prepared to act swiftly from a central point. That, of course, and is Berlin. It must also have a trained and well-oiled network of spies backed up by all the latest technological advances. That' what the new BND complex will hold.

Chancellor Merkel, thinks, *How appropriate and timely such a new complex is,* as she heads toward a meeting with Germany's new head of intelligence, Walter Kunzman, who already has built up a substantial army of spies and intelligence employees to get the ball rolling, so to say.

The entire question of intelligence and need for a larger pool of spies and undercover operatives came into focus during the recent confrontation with Russia about its natural gas supply. Germany, if not all of Europe, was being blackmailed to cough up bigger Euros for energy.

Energy ... That's what it was all about ... energy. Not so much Euros or dollars. She smiled as she thought of how the dollar was dropping in value against the Euro -- the fresh new currency in the world that was only born some six years ago. Already it was inching ahead of the almighty U.S. dollar. *It was simply because of confidence,* she thinks and smiles to herself. It is impossible for her not to flash back to the times when the dollar was king in the world. The Euro didn't exist, and the Deutsche Mark was two to one, or even four to one, going back to her youth, but never mind that. She is more concerned with the question of what really drives the global economy. It is not the international monetary fund, the federal reserve. It's not old oil or any other commodity. Sure as hell, its not the traders. It is confidence, confidence in the country behind the currency. She loves America and is grateful for everything it had done for her country since World War II, but it is no secret that investors all over the world were beginning to pull away from the shaky dollar and rely on a young and upcoming currency -- the Euro.

Right now, as she enters the Bundestag Building, she must concentrate on something even more important for Germany -- the European Union and Energy. Putin, that bastard, will play a deadly game. Simply because he holds new weapons more powerful then the nuclear bomb. Chancellor Merkel is visibly upset with just that thought.

Russia's massive energy and natural gas reserves are overflowing. Oil, natural gas, uranium, gold, copper, silver, zinc -- all those are Putin's new control weapon and he will know how to use it. Once KGB, always KGB. She is livid just at the though of it.

She has reached Kunzman's office and conference room. She enters a meeting of several cabinet members and Kunzman is already speaking. The half dozen men stand politely until the Chancellor has taken her seat at the head of the oval conference table.

"This late, and unexpected meeting, gentlemen, I am given to understand is most urgent and involves our ally the United States." She waits patiently for someone to speak.

There are no files, documents or writing pads anywhere on the large table.

"Ms's Chancellor," Kunzman begins. He is a man in his late forties, with premature white hair and an energetic hawkish face. "We have some information from our operatives in the U.S."

"It must be top secret and surely out of the ordinary for you to ask me here?"

"It is," Kunzman replies. "The Roswell rumors may be more than rumors. Two Interpol agents are dead as well as four of Putin's men. Our men have not interfered as a courtesy to the CIA and your relationship with the president.

"I would hope not," Merkel replies sternly. Then, as an afterthought, Merkel asks, "Why would we? The Roswell matter is their business. Why should that blunder be of our concern?"

Kunzman smiles. "Because, Ms. Chancellor, a reliable source direct from the Pentagon informed us that our theory on that particular matter since the late fifties may be true."

"Why? Why would Russia and Interpol risk its men on U.S. soil? If it is the usual flying disc cover-up?" Kunzman states.

Merkel is slightly impatient. "I wouldn't know. I was never fully briefed on this affair, in office or before."

"Granted," Kunzman states. "There was no urgency then and, for that matter, until now, until we received this recent information. Our theory was, and is now, that a parallel to the Penemunde experience is occurring."

"Ach bitte, Herr Kunzman, not World War II science fiction again."

Kunzman stands ready to make his point. "We know, as a fact, that Werner von Braun was assisted by someone whose identity was never established by any agency, ever, while preparing the first U.S. space probe for NASA.

"Please, Kunzman get to the point," Merkel says, irritated, but willing to hear all the details.

"Very well. If our information is correct, the United States may be in possession of an energy source that will make Russia's resources pale."

Kunzman sits and looks at a silent chancellor.

Finally, and, after long thought, Merkel breaks the silence. "What are you suggesting? That a close and very friendly relationship be maintained with the United States?"

"Right now, Ms. Chancellor, China and our European Union are vying for Russia's energy sources. If America takes the lead through this incredible occurrence, we will be well served to stand on its side."

Twenty minutes later, over a beer in a quiet, small bistro in Berlin, Chancellor Merkel cannot help ask Kunzman about Penemunde, the birthplace of the V-1 and V-2 rockets developed by Werner von Braun.

Kunzman is just too happy to explain. "Von Braun was not alone. The few documents recovered, and in our archives, definitively indicate that there was an individual involved who has never been identified by anyone, one that simply disappeared, but, reappeared with Von Braun at Cape Canaveral."

Merkel smiles faintly: "OK. Your theory, whatever, Fliegende Untertassen (flying saucers)?"

"We have proof of such phenomenon over our skies, long before the occurrences in America's Roswell. But, as you know, Hitler demanded silence just like the Americans. Hush was the word. No media to report anything. Then, it was nothing but rumors because der Fuhrer wanted it that way."

"All right, Kunzman, you have made your point. I only hope that we have the right man in charge of our intelligence."

Deep inside Merkel is relieved and jumping for joy so to say. Although she does not fully understand or know anything about this energy source. From what she does understand, she could take a much firmer position with that SOB Putin. *It would be great for the EU to be able to tell him to just "Shove it."*

Chapter 73

At the Adventure Mine, the same crew of people who had earlier lowered the container of goods into the mine shaft 1,500 feet below ground are now laboring to hoist it back to the surface. In the frenzy to retrieve the goods, they are oblivious to the burring noise outside and the sound of a Marine Corps helicopter that has landed in the mining complex parking lot area, not until they are confronted by a squad of camouflaged marine commandos do they realize that they have company.

The Marine Colonel who identifies himself as Colonel Bocker simply asks, "A. Smith," looking at the group of men carrying the container with the goods.

One of the society members steps forward. "Colonel Bocker, William O'Reilley.
You won't find Smith here but he asked me to tell you that he did what he had to do and the goods are yours. Smith still has matters to take care of."

"Very well," Bocker nods and gestures to his men to take charge of the goods which are quickly transported to the chopper, blades still rotating and ready for take of.

Williams turns back to his Society members with a smile. "I hope they know what to do with it . We got what we wanted. Mission accomplished."

The members exit from the mine just as the helicopter is disappearing behind the distant tree line.

Chapter 74

Evan and Amber step off the Midwest Commuter plane that has just landed at the Gogebic County Airport, Ironwood, Michigan, located fifty miles west of the little village called Light Struck, Michigan. As they disembark from the aircraft, they are met by a man in plain clothes, who identifies himself as officer Gilman of the Michigan State Patrol, briefly flashing his ID badge and inquiring, "Mr. Kirkland?"

Evan nods. "In person," he acknowledges while letting his overnight bag drop to the ground.

Gilman picks up the nylon overnighter and reaches for Amber's baggage as well. "Right over here, sir." He gestures to a set of two Michigan State Patrol cars parked near the plane on the tarmac. One vehicle is fully marked with a uniformed driver waiting at the wheel. The other, a dark blue unmarked sedan with one, single, nearly unnoticeable antenna protruding from the center of the roof. Officer Gilman proceeds to the trunk of the unmarked squad car and deposits the baggage into it and proceeds to open the driver's door to explain a few things to this very important couple from Washington. "The vehicle is fully equipped, Mr. Kirkland. Fully automated GPS system and computerized communications system with access to anywhere." Gilman leans into the car, pointing out something on the dashboard. "The small blue button next to the dial and speaker system activates a tracking system and you're on our radar screen. Once you activate that we are practically on top of you."

Amber cannot help remarking. "Well, I certainly hope that won't be necessary."

"Anything else?" Evan inquires.

"There is plenty of firepower in there for any emergency."

Amber moves to the passenger side of the car. As she comes around the front end of the vehicle, she looks again and cannot help but once again remarks. "You see, I told you Michigan would be a fun place." With a smile, she quickly gets into the car.

While Evan is used to her sense of humor, Gilman hasn't a clue of what she is talking about as he starts to move toward the waiting marked squad. "Let me know if there is anything you'll be needing, sir."

Thank you for all your help," Evan replies and slides behind the wheel of the sedan. Once inside the vehicle, Amber hands him two newspapers that have been left there specifically for Evan and Amber to see upon their arrival. One is the Detroit Press, the other the Michigan Globe, a rural Upper Peninsula daily publication.

The front page headlines on both papers are the same.

Government admits to 60-year UFO cover up.

While Evan starts the car and heads out to the highway, Amber reads aloud. "The Air Force admits that the Project Blue Book reports and conclusions were fabricated, perpetrated for reasons of national security."

Evan chuckles. "What else? It has to be for national security reasons. Everything the government does is for the good of the people. We must keep the sheep safe at all costs."

Amber keeps glancing at the articles but thinks out loud at the same time. "Well prepared and written ... Basically, it admits everything but says very little. The spin put on this is precious," she concludes. "The Defense Department will make every effort to thoroughly research its files to discover the truth of the entire Roswell Incident and get to the bottom of it all." She continues to read out loud. "The president and the Secretary of Defense Runsfeld, feel that the people have the right to know everything."

"This is good," Evan voices, sarcastically. "They are going to lay the blame on the administration in charge then, half a century ago and everyone in between they can think of."

"But the Freedom of Information Act and such inquiring minds as the Star Light Society will keep digging," Amber shoots back.

"Listen," Evan says. "If the Senate and Congress agree and nobody starts any hearings, this whole thing will disappear into oblivion. They cannot afford to let this smolder, let alone catch on fire."

Amber looks at him. "There will always be

leaks."

"It doesn't matter," Evan continues. "In this case everything, and I do mean everything, will be overshadowed by what they got in trade for these admissions and headlines. Don't forget that -- an energy source that can change life on earth forever. Do you think anyone will care about a cover-up? If life changes for the better, hell no."

The vehicle Evan is driving is traveling east now on the remote and desolate section of Interstate Highway 2, the one northern highway that connects the country from east to west.

Amber is still studying every line of the news article. She turns sideways to face him in the drivers seat. "There is nothing mentioned in here about the bodies, the missing alien or the autopsy for that matter. Isn't that what the Star Lighters wanted? To get that out into the open and made public?"

Evan, concentrating on his driving, glances at Amber. "Shatzie, think for a second. There has to be a balance. Our mission is part of that. Think about public outcry and demands, everybody shouting and demanding, "We want to see an alien, an extraterrestrial. They don't even know what to expect or know what is real, what is science fiction or science fact. Knowledge is not what they are seeking but sensationalism." Evan pulls the car off the road onto the shoulder, putting it into park, then fully turns toward Amber. "They, the public, wouldn't be satisfied until they saw a little green man. Or, the carcasses of the ones put on ice. Frozen, as only we know they still exist. Would they even understand, or comprehend, the fact that extraterrestrials can take on different life forms? I know that's far out. Everyone expects to see little green men from Mars. What a disappointment to the world-at-large if our aliens weren't green and didn't have big oval eyes that glow in the dark. Shit, nobody would even understand what we're talking about.

Amber is taking it all in and attempting to compute it in her mind to make sense of it. "You are making sense but you're also talking Washington talk. Don't tell all; cover it up; it's for the good of the people."

"Yeah, with one difference, Shatzie. We are not politicians or lawyers," Evan intones "We are not and don't want to be. Yes, we do know what it is all about but all we can do is be guided by logic, common sense and our personal values. Not to mention purpose, and what is the purpose of it all?"

Amber has listened carefully and can only agree. "I know, I know what you are saying makes sense. I just have not thought about where to draw the line. Besides, who are we to do so ... draw the line, I mean. We are not God. But worst of all we work for the government.."

"I don't know about you, Shatzie, but all my life I have done my job well and not violated my own values and beliefs. Like you, I investigated, researched, compiled and correlated millions of pieces of paper. After that, what the powers to be did with them, I was not told. Actually, I am kind of glad that neither of us has been asked to draw the line."

"You made your point," Amber looks at him in a calm way. "So, what about our mission?"

"Now that, Shatzie, is a good one and you are about to get a shocking answer."

"Shoot," she snaps back.

"We could well become the only people, or at least, be one of a handful of human beings, that have an opportunity to have an encounter of the fifth kind."

Evan looks at Amber. "Yes, if we can find him. At least we know, or think we know, that he is not little nor is he green." Having said that, he starts the car and pulls back onto the road.

Chapter 75

The light over the Bed & Breakfast Lodge is the only illumination casting a faint glow on the green Ford Explorer parked before the entrance, where it stood when it first arrived several weeks ago. Arturo Smith, dressed in a dark blue overcoat and aluminum suitcase in hand, he leaves the lodge and gets into the vehicle.

A curtain parts from the inside dining room window which provides a clear view of the parking area and the driveway dominated by darkness. Eleanor and Gail are watching the departure of Arturo Smith, their ominous and strange guest. "This has been a once-in-a-lifetime experience," Eleanor sighs. "Who else could claim anything of the kind. I will miss him."

"So will I," Gail replies. "Where do you suppose he is going?"

"Who knows? A better place? A distant planet? One thing I am sure of," Eleanor states with conviction. "I am sure he will be just fine wherever he goes."

Gail suddenly has to air a silly thought that comes to her mind as she watches Arturo Smith getting into the car as if nothing unusual has happened. "Mother, he just doesn't look or act like a ..." She pauses turning to face her mother. "... an alien. Just look at him leaving like any guest of ours does. Nothing seems different about him. Are we absolutely sure, Mother, that all of this was real?"

As seen from the window, the Explorer is backing up and turns toward the exit of the drive-way and the road. Slowly it accelerates and disap-pears into the darkness with only the taillights glow-ing ominously until there is nothing.

"Gail, darling?" Eleanor turns to her daugh-ter, closing the curtains. "I can assure you, dear. Everything was just too real. I think it's time for you to read your grandmother's diary. At the same time, maybe everything we have experienced should be forgotten and certainly not talked about because nobody would ever believe it anyway."

Gail is still confused and searching her own mind for how to relate to the entire encounter as a whole. She cannot even write about it. In the process, she parts the curtain one more time, staring into the darkness.

"You are right mother. Nobody would believe us, would they?" She is about to reclose the curtain when she reacts to a set of car headlights coming towards the lodge out of the darkness. "Mother, our Mr. Smith is coming back."

Eleanor stands next to her daughter and sees the vehicle approaching. "Why would he come back? Did he forget something?   Wait. that's not his car, Gail, it's another car.   We are certainly not expecting any guests. Now who could that be?"

A dark blue sedan, with the almost undetect-able antenna on its roof, stops in front of the entrance. Evan Kirkland exits from the unmarked state patrol car and moves toward the stairs and the entrance door of the lodge.

Both Eleanor and Gail move down the hall toward the foyer to greet the stranger. The door bell rings but Kirkland does not have to wait long for the door to open.

"Mrs. Madsen?" Evan inquires politely.

"Yes, I'm Eleanor Madsen." She stares questioningly.

Evan understands that an unannounced visit on someone will need some clarification. "My name is Evan Kirkland, Ms. Madsen. I work for the Department of Defense." He hands her a business card and flashes a plastic encased ID card for her to see.

"My goodness, what could I possibly help you with?" Eleanor mutters. "But do come in, Mr. Kirkland."

Amber has joined Evan at the entrance and introduces her. "My associate, Miss Amber Winslow."

The women exchange brief greetings, as Eleanor gestures to them to step inside where they stand in the confines of the small foyer.

"Ms. Madsen," Evan addresses her, "we understand you have a house guest, a Mr. A. Smith. We would very much like to visit with him, if you don't mind."

Eleanor maintains her composure, even though she knows what this all means. "I am afraid we will not be able to help you. You see, Mr. Smith just left.

You probably past him in the driveway as you came in."

Evan and Amber are shocked, but remain calm and seem unaffected by the news. "He's not returning?" Evan asks.

"I don't believe so. His time here was up and he simply checked out.

Amber interjects. "I don't suppose you would know where he was going from here?

"I'm afraid not," Eleanor replies stubbornly.

Suddenly, Evan seems rushed. "Should he return Ms. Madsen, please ask him to call us. You have my card."

"I certainly will, Mr. Kirkland. I certainly will."

Evan makes to leave. "Sorry to have disturbed you, but we must be going. Thank you very much, Ms. Madsen." He reaches for the door, turns with a nod and a thanks her.

"No problem, no problem at all." With that she closes the door behind them and sighs with relief.

Evan has no sooner positioned himself behind the wheel when he turns to Amber. "There went our encounter of the fifth kind. What kind of car was that?"

Amber fastens her seat belt. "A green SUV. Couldn't tell what make."

Evan starts the car, ready to turn it around with a ray of hope to maybe catch up with Smith's SUV, a hope quickly fading, realizing that they haven't a clue which direction on the highway Smith turned. Evan impulsively reaches for the communications button. He dials in a 2-digit number code and is immediately connected via speaker phone to the Michigan State Patrol.

"Gilman here," echoes the voice through the car.

Evan responds. "Our subject is driving a late-model green SUV. Don't know the make or plate number. What can you do for us? Our subject left the Bed & Breakfast Lodge about 20 to 25 minutes ago. We have no idea what direction he went. We will be driving south on Highway 45."

"Don't worry, Mr. Kirkland. We have you on the radar screen. We will call you back as soon as we get word."

At the State Patrol Headquarters in Wakefield, Michigan, an all point bulletin is dispatched to all cars in the southwestern area of the Upper Peninsula.

Chapter 76

The Star Trek set designers would be envious of the room situated in a new underground facility near Colorado Springs. The government has designated this location as the new Area 51. Stainless steel and glass form the octagon-shaped control room walls which serve as the primary advanced weapons technology laboratory for the United States Air Force.

Two-star General Brad Christoferson, in charge of the newly occupied facility, is nervously pacing the floor, circling a freestanding work table on top of which lies a perfect crystal sphere, bluish-silver in color, not much larger then an ordinary basket- ball. The general's restless moves are being watched carefully by an older, white-haired gentleman engrossed in working a computer keyboard streamlined into a huge operating console of some sort that could easily be mistaken as Captains Kirk's new command desk on the Enterprise.

Professor Janush Pidim is one of the most brilliant scientists the United States government has had at its disposal since World War II. Estonian of national origin, he was taken off the hands, so to say, of the KGB during the Cold War when the Baltic countries were still living under the grip of communist rule. Taking credit for the stealth navigating system and other weaponry marvels, he is now in charge of something he has never dealt with before.

X-rays, digital scans, laser bombardment, and pressure tests of various kinds have failed to penetrate it, open it or provide a single clue of what is contained in that mysterious sphere, which is supposed to hold the secret to all energy needs on this planet.

The general places his hands on the sphere. "So, professor, now what?"

"Not to panic. I am surprised, however, that our friend Arturo has not given us something to work with." Pidim pushes a button on the console as he turns and moves to the center of the room, joining the general, gazing at the steel ball. "There can only be one thing that holds the secret. Something we have not tried or even considered."

"What, Janush?" the general asks, taking his hand off the sphere.

"Thought, my friend. Simply, thought."

The general is visibly confused.

"The energy may respond to mind over matter, General. Completely different than what we have applied so far. I will work If one would only know this Smith better. It would help solve this puzzle.

As the general moves to take a seat in front of this unusually large contraption. "Janush." He addresses the professor in a soft voice. "How in the hell do we handle this. You know what I mean."

Professor Pidim dips into a tray of jelly beans, pops one into his mouth and takes a seat behind the console before he answers the general. "We don't do anything. Just keep performing the tests as ordered. We know the sphere, or ball, whatever you want to call it, cannot be opened and used right now. So, we keep it that way until we know for sure if all prerequisites are met."

The general nods in agreement but is visually more uncomfortable. "You're sure you can't get a hold of Smith?"

Pidim shakes his head. "I am sure. Even if I could, you know as well as I do, it wouldn't do any good right now, would it?" He looks at the general and smiles.

Chapter 77

The little village of Light Struck, Michigan is experiencing something very special. A State Patrol Car Convention. Squad cars with, and without their lights flashing and sirens wailing have been circulating in all directions for over an hour now, arriving and departing to and from a lone unmarked car parked in front of the Bardo's Cafe, occupied by Evan and Amber, who are anxiously waiting for some results in the effort to find the mysterious Mr. Smith.

Fifteen miles south of Light Struck a green Ford Explorer has been parked in the parking lot of the Lac View Desert Casino for over an hour.

After searching and crisscrossing every main road and side road for over an hour in a 50-mile radius of Light Struck, did the State Patrol think of having the Indian police check their casino parking lot 15 miles down the road for the wanted SUV. Sure as hell, there it was, parked smack right in front of the main casino entrance.

Ten minutes after the find, and the vehicle is reported to Evan and Amber, 20 State Patrol cars arrive, followed a minute later by Evan and Amber. The Lac View Desert Casino is transformed instantly into a chaotic battleground. The fully armed State Troopers, with a variety of firepower, have a disruptive effect on the five hundred or more gamblers in attendance at the casino. Before even barricades at the respective entrances and exits can be set up hundreds of people are fleeing in an attempt to avoid being in the crossfire of any possible fireworks.

This well intended, but chaotic effort by the State Patrol, turns up no Mr. Smith, and has resulted in panicking one hell of a lot of people and losing the casino a half or so million. It takes another hour to bring everything under control.

State troopers report to Evan that the vehicle Smith was driving is a Hertz rental leased by a Arthur Collins at the Rhinelander, Wisconsin airport the same day Smith arrived in the Upper Peninsula of Michigan. This would all make sense. Rhinelander is about an hour drive from Light Struck and the Bed & Breakfast Lodge.

But then again, why would Smith need a car at all? Does this make any sense, Evan thinks to himself, trying to put it all together in his mind, especially since a thorough search of the entire casino complex has turned out to be a total disaster. They have drawn a blank.

Chapter 78

Washington, D.C.

Runsfeld is on the telephone with General Christoferson. The information he is receiving will call for another high-level meeting at the oval office. He can only bark into the speaker phone. "You have the best we got at your disposal, get on it and figure it out." Pushing the off button as he stands angrily, he leaves his office.

Chapter 79

Evan and Amber are exhausted as they enter her apartment. Not so much from the trip to the Upper Peninsula of Michigan but from the five-hour debriefing session at the Pentagon about their unsuccessful journey to solve all the problems. At the same time, they were told about the mystery sphere which at that moment was good for nothing and infuriating everyone from the bottom of the ladder to the oval office.

The mystery reminds Evan of the aluminum foil story, a material discovered at the Roswell crash site. One could crumple it up into a small ball and it would unfold itself to its previous natural shape. What was it? Mystery never solved. Sure as hell, however, the whole thing was covered up. Evan, himself, had a piece of that material in his hand at one time. If it hadn't been for that fact, he would not have become a believer.

Amber is behind the breakfast counter mixing a salad and, as if reading Evan's thoughts, asks, "What about that other extraterrestrial, the one Dan Garder makes all the fuss about. Is he real?"

"That's real all right -- maybe a different species of alien also it's from a different crash in Texas."

"But he, or it, are still in custody?" Amber inquires.

"Don't know. I was out of the whole affair

long before this Smith thing surfaced and you came into the picture."

"So, what are you saying?" she keeps digging.

"I don't know how credible this Garder guy is. I never examined his files or met him."

"Don't you think we should do that, especially since nobody knows what to do with that thing. This is one mystery that needs solving.

"Garder was, and maybe still is, a government employee with a top secret rating. According to what I remember and the current internet spin, he has had continuous conversations with the entity who, I understand, and this is unconfirmed, is the kind of extraterrestrial the world at large would expect to see."

"Kind of green, spindly and with big oval glowing eyes of no doubt," Amber cannot help remarking.

"Not quite, but close enough, according to Dan Gaders descriptions and the stories he's put out."

Amber has served the salad and places the plates on the dinette table so Evan, as usual, sits opposite her and both have a view through the big picture window of the street that runs through a quiet, elegant neighborhood of Washington. "Sit down and rest your brain."

"All right, all right," Evan mumbles, as he attempts to correlate yet another stack of papers spread out over the cocktail table and on the couch. Ever since they have expressed their affection toward each other, Evan has been spending more and more time at Amber's apartment and often spent the nights there. Their appreciation for each others talents and abilities was not only mutual but rewarding and full of purpose. They shared so many common interests, not just professional interests, but philosophical and moral and political. Amber does not have to remind him again. Evan drops the whole bundle of papers back on the couch, mumbling. "To hell with it," and takes his seat at the table opposite that gorgeous creature he is head-over-heels in love with.

"Water chestnuts," he mumbles. "Nice touch for a salad. I like that."

"Refreshing, I thought," she says. "So what now, Mr. Kirkland? How does this great energy source work? What do we do next?"

Evan looks up at her and smiles. "Question one: What now, Mr. Kirkland? Mr. Kirkland could make an excellent suggestion." He looks at her teasingly.

Amber smiles, knowing exactly what he means.

He continues. "Question number two: How does the gadget work? Let them figure it out, we're not scientists. As to question number three: What do we do now? Let's go back to answer number one."

"   Would you like your lamb chops now while they are hot?" Amber has finished her salad and rises with her empty plate in hand, ready to serve dinner.

"I'll take anything that's hot, Schatzie."

"Restrain yourself, Mr. Kirkland." As Amber

places the dinner plate with piping hot and brown perfectly, broiled lamb chops in front of him, then serves herself.

As she has done before, she has served up another gourmet dinner effortlessly in a short period of time. From the first time they had dined together at her apartment, she has been precise as all hell about how everything is served. He has always been amazed with the detail and care with which she prepared their meals. In this case, the mint jelly is neatly placed on a thin orange slice on top of each broiled lamb chop, sautéed thin sliced beans with equally thin slices of almonds are neatly place next to the chops and the small serving of brown, halved, young red potatoes. Any man would kill for a meal and a woman like this.

At the same time, she enjoys his delight in her cooking and appreciation of her detailed efforts. Quietly they enjoy the meal until Evan feels he must voice a compliment. after taking his first bite. "You outdid yourself again Shatzie. Out of this world."

She looks at him directly and sheepishly and asks with a faint smile. "Dessert?"

Evan's eyes light up. The door bell rings. They look at each other in surprise.

"Expecting someone?" Evan asks.

"Never when I am with Mr. Kirkland," she replies. The door bell rings again. "Maybe I should answer it." She unwillingly moves to the door and opens it.

The man standing at the doorstep politely

inquires.   "I am looking for Mr. Kirkland and Ms. Winslow. My name is Smith, Arturo Smith.

Evan jumps up from the chair like a rocket. "The 'Mr. Smith' we have been looking for?"

"Or maybe the Mr. Smith that has been looking for you," comes the answer.

"Please, come in," Amber almost unintentionally elevating her voice.

Evan shows Arturo Smith to the table as Amber closes the door behind her, follows them and proceeds to clear off what is left on the table. Smith sits down.

"Coffee or tea, Mr. Smith," she asks. "Or maybe a drink?"

"Coffee will be fine. Thank you," Smith retorts.

"Mr. Smith," Evan begins. "This is an unexpected event. How did you find us?"

"Shall we say with the help of computer technology," he answers, a faint smile on his face.

"Why us?" Evan continues. "As you may know there are a few people waiting to meet you."

"I am aware of that. Everything has its place and time. I am aware of the work you are doing and your efforts to reach me and please call me Arturo."

"Arturo," Amber injects "You know there is a problem with the -- " She searches for the right word. "The gadget, this energy source our government received."

"Of course," he replies. "I am also aware that the Star Light Society has been, as you put it, 'duped' by your government."

Amber stands and quickly pours a cup of coffee for Smith. "There is a bit of confusion and problems over how this gadget works."

"I am well aware of that," Smith states sternly.

Evan looks at him. "Mr. Smith, we are told the source cannot be opened or accessed. The president is very frustrated, I understand."

Arturo takes a sip of coffee. "That is why I am here, Mr. Kirkland. While I can tell you how it works, the use of the energy source may be restricted for a time."

"I don't understand." Both Amber and Evan are puzzled.

Smith, however, comes right to the point. "Inside the   sphere, as you call it, are literary billions of granules, energy granules if you will. Each granule in your measurements is two millimeters in diameter. Injected into an existing atomic reactor, it is equivalent to hundreds or more kilograms of uranium fuel. It is like splitting the atom again and again. The results are continuous energy production."

"Good, God," Evan exclaims. "That's incredible, if I understand it correctly."

"So, there is a solution to our problems?" Amber questions.

"Yes, and no," Smith comes back.
Amber and Evan look at each other questioningly.

"I'm afraid we don't know what you mean."

"Your government is in possession of it but

using it is not yet possible."

"Why?" Evan's and Amber's voice echo at the same time.

"Mr. Kirkland and Ms. Winslow, I am familiar with your backgrounds. You will understand why your country is not ready. Your politicians are not ready for this nor are the people or your private enterprise system -- your monopolies as some refer to them," Smith continues. "Unlimited sources of energy bring with it great power. Power, if not used wisely and fairly, can be dangerous to the entire planet. By asking your government to disclose the truth about Roswell the Star Light Society imposed a test on it, a test to determine if it was ready to act responsibly. The hope was that it would be ready to do the right thing without more wars, without concern for profits, without the pain that will come as energy runs out."

Evan stands. He is getting frustrated. "I know what you are saying but, I sure as hell would not want to be the one telling this to the president, nor the secretary of defense of the United States."

"Please, Mr. Kirkland do not be concerned. The Society will tell your government when the time is right."

"That's a calming thought."

"Look around you, Mr. Kirkland. You are fighting wars on two fronts that may escalate to unstoppable proportions, if not end in self-destruction. In the process other nations will become involved. Sooner or later the nuclear button, as you refer to it, will be pushed."

"Not a pretty picture, Mr. Smith." Evan says, sitting down again, deep in thought.

Amber is taking everything in, getting the message loud and clear.

"Unfortunately, that is not all. The same problem exists with other nations. Who would you trust, Mr. Kirkland? To be in charge of this energy source?"

Evan shrugs, giving thorough thought to his question. "Damned, you are right, Mr. Smith. I wouldn't know who to trust."

"Certainly not our politicians," Amber blurts out.

"Now you know why I am here. It is a problem. Is it not?"

Evan changes the subject. "How does the Star Light Society fit into this picture?"

"They can be trusted. A very devoted group of individuals. Certainly not radical, militant or aggressive. On the contrary, rather passive and conservative in their beliefs. Truth is only a detriment when dealing with people who don't believe in truth."

"So, what is the solution, Mr. Smith?" Amber asks.

"I was prepared for you to ask that," Smith calmly replies. "Put the government to the test."

Evan and Amber exchange a look of slight confusion. "And just how do you envision that?"

Smith smiles and stands up halfway to reach into his side coat pocket from which he extracts a silver packet and from this he extracts a capsule no larger then a large vitamin pill. He places it on the center of the table. It indeed resembles a one-inch long, cod liver oil casule, except for its grayish steel color. "This contains enough energy granules to put your government to the test, so to say. It is yours to do with as you deem proper."

"Why us?" Amber and Evan blurt out at the same time.

"We trust you."

Cautiously, Evan fingers the capsule, realizing it is hard like steel.

"Careful in opening it," Smith warns. "It slides apart. The granules are very small. Your scientists will know what to do and how to test it. It will also eliminate the creation of all future waste from your nuclear power plants. You have already buried enough in underground waste storage facilities to induce the China syndrome some day soon. We wish to avoid that at any cost."

Amber paces the floor in an open area around the dinner table. "And if this is used wisely by our government, then what?"

Evan cuts in. "And what party do we trust?"

Smith smiles again. He fully realizes the situation and the predicament he has placed them in. "There is enough material here," he points to the capsule, "to last through two administrations. If the powers that be cannot find a way to cooperate with each other and create harmony and peace amongst themselves and all other world leaders, then the large, primary energy source your government now has in its possession, will not work for them. It simply will never be opened.

"Mr. Smith," Amber begins, sitting down and facing him. "Do you realize we could get killed over this? Besides, the CIA and the Bureau are still looking for you."

"I am quite aware of that," Smith states calmly, "but, please, do not concern yourself with me. I will be fine."

Evan is curious. "Arturo? How is it, you simply disappeared from the radar screen, like a few days ago in Michigan when we came to see you?"

Smith leans back after taking a sip of coffee and seems suddenly to enjoy this conversation and his company's bewilderment. "I did not just disappear, physically that is. You just could not see me. Neither did the State Patrol, right? True, one cannot see if the mind does not allow it."

"May I ask you something else?" Evan has to inquire.

"I am at your disposal."

"From what I have read in our files, you have consistently been of help to the government before this -- the stealth project, Start Wars, NASA and advanced weaponry projects. Why now?"

"I don't understand?" Smith replies, slightly confused.

"Why not give them what you have directly. Why us?"

"Mr. Kirkland, surely you can understand that if I remained I would be kept here and asked, if not forced, to perform more services until they have everything they want." Smith seems repulsed by that thought, shaking his head. "I have done enough. Yourpolitics are such that I would be under constant pressure. There's the risk of exposure, leaving much too much to explain. Even the Society would no longer be able to assist and protect me. He pauses. "The time has come for your government to sort things out for themselves."

Amber is compelled to reply with her usual dry humorous sarcasm in her voice, "We all know that will never happen. They'll kill each other with venom first, if not physically, before they are happy."

Smith nods understandingly. "I have been here for quite some time -- 60 some years in your time frame. This country of yours was a different place all together then. I have witnessed the deterioration in every aspect of life since then." He pauses. "We are not happy."

"What do you mean by 'we'?"

Smith continues. "It is a very large universe that surrounds this small speck in the system. You are not alone. One creator rules all. However, whatever you wish to believe is yours alone to decide." He again pauses for a moment. "But when the actions of one civilization and one life form can affect all others, everyone becomes concerned, as does the creator of it all -- God."

"That's a profound mouthful, Mr. Smith," Evan thoughtfully replies

Chapter 80

The steel capsule is being held up against a halogen quartz desk light, between index finger and thumb belonging to Professor Janush Pidim. The professor and General Christoferson are alone in the darkened main control room at the Colorado top secret experimental weapons facility.

The capsule was delivered to them from the Defense Department with the instruction test its worth immediately.

"They should have sent Smith, alias Collins, alias Schweitzer, with it." Pidim mumbles. "These developments put us into a very precarious position, as you well know," carefully placing the capsule on the smooth, glassy surface of the huge console desk area.

"You're talking about our man, I take it." The general fingers the capsule delicately as if it were loaded with nitroglycerin.

Pidim smiles at the general, then takes the capsule and pounds it on the desktop. "It wont explode, I assure you. It's of the same material as our thus far useless steel ball. Any ideas?"

"Maybe. The only instruction I was given. Follow orders. Place the contents of this in the fuel container of a nuclear reactor. It is to replace the uranium fuel rod. Any nuclear reactor or power plant will do."

Pidim picks up the capsule again and gradually twists both ends of the capsule in opposite directions. "Ah, ha,... there is some play in here." Very slowly he continues to manipulate both ends of the capsule carefully holding it up vertically so as not to spill any content if there is separation."

The general looks on with anxious anticipation. The capsule separates into two parts, the hull making up the upper part is empty, while the lower part holds tiny glass like granules about as small as the shot loaded in a 38 or 45 caliber pistol bird-shot cartridge. The general leans over to get a closer look. "That's it? What do you make of it?"

Pidim, now, carefully replaces the empty hull portion of the capsule back over the one filled with the granules. "I have worked with our man on Stealth and two other projects. He's not only real, but always right on the mark. You can be sure of that. "Would you be good enough to reach Fitzgerald at the Atomic Energy Commission. we need to visit a nuclear power plant. Which one? I don't care. Only Class 12-A cleared personnel at our disposal. This could take some time. These elements are so small I don't know how in the hell they would replace a full-sized fuel rod. "Oh," Pidim voices as an afterthought. "If you have to get Fitzgerald out of bed don't hesitate."

Chapter 81

"No, Mr. President. Smith simply disappeared." It is the middle of the night. Runsfeld and the president are alone in the oval office.

"What the hell is the use. You, at least, can resign under pressure. But I can't. How can we fail on all fronts?"

"Smith was never controllable. He always came and went as he pleased. Kirkland said he showed up unexpectedly, handed over the test material, gave them lot of mumbo jumbo about peace on earth. Said good bye."

"And disappeared into thin air, no doubt," the president remarks, sarcastically. "And what if this stuff doesn't work?"

"General Christoferson and Pidim are at the nuclear facility as we speak."

"Damn, why in the hell couldn't we get Smith to be there at least for this?"

"We have no way of finding him him. You know this is ironic. Our entire intelligence and military system cannot keep track of one man."

"Sometimes, yes. Sometimes, no," Runsfeld intones.

"I am told that the process of testing the sample will take at least 48 hours to determine how to replace fuel rods with something so small."

"We have the best we got on it -- Eisenberg,

Steiner and Wallace -- our cream-of-the-crop scientists, not to forget Pidim. They'll figure it out."

"And if they don't?" The president looks straight at Runsfeld and with a firm, angry voice. "If they don't, we have nothing to throw into the election that would make the difference. Do you understand that?"

"Oh, Mr. President, that's something Kirkland brought up. Smith wanted to see some unity amongst the parties and world leaders. He keeps talking about peace and harmony amongst the left and right as well as the world powers."

The President jumps out of his chair. "Smith wants? Who in hell does he think he is? Is he a total nut case! Sure, I'll just snap my fingers and we have peace on earth just like that. That's impossible and we all damn well know it. We're talking about politics here. Congress, the Senate, Putin, Amadinejad and Bin Laden." The president is pacing the floor with furious steps, his face taking on a reddish color. "Insanity, that's what it is. Sheer nonsense. And it's not that we don't try but we have Putin holding the worlds largest resources -- natural gas reserves, minerals, oil, uranium and gold, in his hands. That's leverage and he knows how to use it ... the European Union, the next Holy Roman Empire a foregone conclusion -- with the Euro getting stronger and stronger by the day against our dollar. Where in the hell do I start? Not to mention China, and I don't want to go there." He practically falls into his chair and hopelessly admits, "No resolve on the Middle East front, damn Iraq, and this idiot, Smith, want's peace? Just like that. And how do we get there? With a mysterious capsule, or a crystal ball we can't open -- science fiction bullshit."

Runsfeld attempts to restore some calm. "Surely, Mr. President, Smith does not expect instant, overnight results. Maybe he is testing our will to make change?"

"That's wonderful." The president jumps out of his chair again. "Testing our will? With my national approval rating at an all-time low and the world sees us as an aggressor, the Ugly American, and I should just make peace? What the hell does everyone think I've been trying to do? Those Democratic dick heads!"

"That's what they are saying about us," Runsfeld interjects.

"Right," the president snaps back. "And that's what's wrong. Everything is a pissing match."

"Kirkland made a profound remark to me, Mr. President -- something Smith said to Kirkland. We can't change anything in the world unless we first change ourselves."

"And what other wisdom did this idiot bestow on your man Kirkland?"

"Why don't you ask him yourself?"

"Since we don't have Smith, go ahead arrange it. The sooner the better."

Chapter 82

The men in white coats fill every open space in the nuclear reactor room of the nuclear power plant near Kenosha, Wisconsin. An entire staff of scientists and technical personnel are assembled for the event of placing a granule from the small capsule into a nuclear fuel container and lowering it into the combustion chamber of the power plant.

A young man in his forties, Seymor Wallace steps up to professor Pidim. "That's not much more then a grain of salt. It will never work."

"Patience Seymor. We 'll find out soon."

Technicians are manning a variety of consoles with gauges and switches too numerous to identify as they begin the process of manipulating the switches to activate the reactor.

One large lever is pushed down by a technician who informs everyone that everything is operational. "All systems are on."

With anxious anticipation the entire flock of white-coated men and woman move to a main operating console with a display of a dozen or more gauges which monitor the functions of the reactor and the power plant operating systems. The technician that dropped the large lever steps up to the console with the gauges and meters.

"It should have fired by now." He turns to his superiors. "Continue, sir, or shut down?" he asks.

There is an instantaneous reaction of bodies turning away from the main console.

"I have power," a loud voice is heard.

Pidim and General Christoferson move up to look at the console and the gauges. Needles are vibrating and wildly quivering. All are showing one hundred percent performance of whatever systems are in operation.

"Something is going on," Pidim says. "Can we have a look at the security camera images?" With that, Pidim and the general move to another section of the room housing a square cluster of digital monitors that display images representing every angle of the nuclear power plant from the outside entrance gate to individual entrance doors to wide shots of the power plant from a substantial distance.

Pidim, the General and everyone around them are amazed as they stare at the wide image of the power plant with the huge disbursement chimney's billowing very clear transparent heated exhaust into the air, a surefire indication that all systems are working and generating power. The plant is fully operational.

Pidim turns to several scientists surrounding him. "Check the air sample and exhaust monitors." Pidim turns back to the General. "You are seeing it with your own eyes, from science fiction to science fact."

The same voice heard previously echoes through the room again. "We are at full power and the output is steady."

Chapter 83

It is early in the day. A tired president stands as he receives Evan Kirkland and Amber Winslow in the oval office. He walks up the them to shake their hands. "Please, be seated." He gestures to a table to the side with four, high-backed Victorian chairs placed around it. A White House waiter enters with a tray of coffee and tea.

"Surely you have been informed that the samples are working, Mr. President. It is somewhat a miracle, our scientists tell us."

"Thank you for all your efforts." They are seated now. The president continues. "So, you are among the few who have met the mysterious Mr. Smith."

"Arturo, he prefers to be called," Amber interjects.

"Arturo," the president repeats. He smiles. "What's he like? What is your impression of him."

"On the surface, nothing unusual about him at all, very intelligent, excellent command of the English language, and most other languages, I understand. Meeting him on the street, he'd be just another person."

"What else did he say about the energy source, the sphere, this ball, or whatever you call it? How do we use it?"

"That he made quite clear, Mr. President." Evan hesitates. "The small capsule was to be a test,

Mr. President, as Arturo put it."

"A test for what?"

Amber feels the need to explain this one. "Arturo thought this country had deteriorated morally and politically considerably since he has been here. He felt there was a need to put it back on track. He also stated with this energy available to this government it would be a way to make changes."

The president raises his eyebrows, then nods. "So, then, in exchange for this energy source he wants me to make changes. What if I cannot accomplish that?"

"As we understand it," Amber says, glancing at Evan to obtain a nod of agreement, then continues, "the small capsule contains enough energy to serve this country through two administrations. If change for the better does not come about, the main source, the sphere, cannot be used. That's pretty much how he put it."

"The president smiles with bittersweet sarcasm. "Two administrations. Hmmm? I wonder why it was put like that?" He muses.

"I guess, Mr. President, he thought that maybe, just maybe, the two parties could consult with each other and reach some common ground to determine what is more important -- politics or energy?"

The president no longer smiles. There is no sarcasm on his face or in his voice. He is dead serious. He nods. "Thank you, Mr. Kirkland, Ms. Winslow. I am afraid much will be up to the American people." He stands, a sign that their meeting with the president of the United States is concluded.

After Evan and Amber leave, a side door in the Oval Office opens and JR enters, the ten-gallon hat cocked at a jaunty angle on top of his head.

"Don't look so down, Georgie boy. This is a win-win situation for us. Sure, it would have been great if he could use this new energy source and could sell it for only half of what we are charging now. With no overhead, we'd make a fortune. Get us out from under those damn rag heads, too. But this is almost as good. We bury the new source and forget where we put it for awhile and still control the old source. Prices can only go up the closer we get to running out. Our best market is still to come."

Chapter 84

General Christoferson answers his cellphone, first checking the caller ID display. "Dave here," he answers, turning his back on the people still gathered in the nuclear power plant facility. "Yes, Mr. Secretary. Absolutely perfect performance." He then listens intently.

The Society wants to make sure they have access to the primary device if all conditions and time frames are not met as required. Do you understand, general?" Asks the voice on the other end of the phone.

"I do, and I will inform Pidim, Senator."

"Good," the senator closes. "The Society must be in control of the source at all times, even if we have possession of it right now. That 's the bottom line."

Chapter 85

It is no more then 24 hours later. Chancellor Merkel of the Bundesrepublic of Germany is on the telephone with the president of the United States. "Mr. President, I understand the problems you face, but I think this Arturo could be right. I think we at least owe it to ourselves to try."

"What about Iran?" the president asks. "What about Russia? What about China? I can't do the impossible. No, this is the best way."

The President smiles. "Thank you Chancellor. I look forward to seeing you tomorrow. Goodbye." He pushes the off button on the speaker phone and muses to himself. *Amazing what energy can do, but what will the next crisis and or conflict be?*

Epilogue

Eight months later.

Evan had tried to convince Amber they should live together. Amber, with her conservative values, would not hear of it. So, it was an informal, small wedding, in a private wedding chapel where they tied the knot of holy matrimony.

It is fall and the most beautiful time of the year in the Upper Peninsula of Michigan. The fall colors are brilliant and a sight to behold when Evan and Amber arrived at Eleanor's Bed & Breakfast Lodge. Both thought it should be a different honeymoon experience than the traditional offerings of tropical paradises or exotic cruises. Making the drive to the north woods of the UP also afforded Amber the opportunity to visit her family in northern Wisconsin and introduce her husband to them.

It was a brief but most pleasant visit. The age difference between Evan and Amber was never an issue. On the contrary, Amber's large family was delighted with Evan and the common interests they shared.

Amber's father, just a bit older then Evan, was also a passionate pipe smoker with a collection of expensive Meerschaum's that made Evan envious. They enjoyed good conversations together, a good smoke, complimented with a good German Cognac.

It was easy for Evan to see and experience first hand where Amber got her talents, good taste and manners. In all, the visit to Amber's family home was one that promised many more visits and family get-togethers.

One of the primary major motivating factors for the newlyweds to visit the Upper Peninsula of Michigan and a honeymoon stay at the Bed and Breakfast Lodge was a promise from Eleanor that she would do everything in her power to have Arturo Smith visit during their stay at the lodge. There was, however, another good reason why they chose to come to Light Struck, Michigan. After Arturo's visit to Amber's apartment in Washington and after their meeting with the president, they decided to become members of the Star Light Society for a variety of personal and philosophical reasons. Subsequently, they had researched their files again and decided to call Eleanor Madsen, who undoubtedly was a member, according to their records. As it turned out, a very important member. Once they belonged to the group, they would be privileged to receive and share information with members, with a solemn oath never to disclose such association or any information about the Society with anyone in the government.

Amber and Evan were resolute that, if such a meeting was to come about, nothing of the meeting would be shared with any of their employers, including Uncle Sam.

At the same time, Eleanor and Gail saw no reason after Amber and Evan joined the society not to make all the necessary contacts for a visit from

Arturo Smith while they were in Light Struck.

Amber, in particular, was anxious to meet Arturo again. After all, how many people   on this planet would ever have an opportunity to meet with an alien, such an articulate, polished being with an intelligence that was hundreds, if not thousands of years, ahead of our time. She and Evan had talked about hundreds of questions that needed to be asked. They had also detected a feeling of sadness in Arturo, signs of vulnerability,   maybe signs of homesickness or yearning to be wherever he belonged. They were not sure. At the same time they pondered over his physical being. Was it all real? Or was it something they -- Amber, Evan and others -- just perceived to be real?

There was only one way to look at this. Maybe they were just not capable of seeing beyond of what was reality somewhere else but not reality on this planet. Nevertheless, they knew, or they thought they knew. One thing was for sure, their hands had touched him and they knew he was flesh and bones as were they.

In the meantime, one of the most intriguing conversation they had was with Eleanor and Gail, was discussing Eleanor's mother's diary. They knew if the contents of that diary were ever made public it would truly be a revelation and blow the top off the White House. The entire Roswell affair would be exposed to the very smallest detail -- the crash, the bodies, the details and findings of the autopsy - every detail - because Eleanor's mother was the surgical nurse at the autopsy of two alien beings, which were nothing like Arturo Smith, inside or outside.

An Interview with Arturo

Arturo Smith, casual as ever, leans back a notch in the leather recliner as he stares at the ceiling, then moves forward again to address a question just asked of him. "I do not find the first eight months of our experiment very promising. The candidates on either side of this predominantly two-party system are not showing signs of being statesmen and healers of a system that is very diseased."

Evan, sitting opposite Arturo Smith on the couch with Amber to his side, feels compelled to comment on Arturo's statement. "But the people really want change and new direction for this country."

"Unfortunately, Mr. Kirkland, the people are spoiled rotten. It's been going on far too long. They are being spoon-fed information and they take it as gospel because they lack education, discipline and an understanding of social economics, to mention just a few flaws. In addition, your society is returning to what your good book refers to as Sodom and Gomorra and becoming an increasingly violent society.

"You are referring to the left and the far left," Evan interjects.

"Not necessarily. You must face the facts. No one on either side is prepared to give up their common and highly antiquated means of transportation, your vehicles, for which, soon, you will have no fuel."

"We are working feverishly on biofuel production all over the world."

"That may not be such a good idea. In the rush to find a solution you use the soil that will be needed for food production to accommodate a population growth you are unwilling control. You simply must understand that your natural resources on this planet are limited. In the meantime, in this country, you are consumed more with the corrupt political process. On one hand the public wants freedoms and less government, less regulations but, on the other hand, when it comes to global warming, as an example you want government to solve the problems of climate change. This is highly contradictory. You do not want restrictive rules but are unwilling to sacrifice the very things that cause the problems. It is the masses and their demands that have caused the problem to begin with."

Arturo pauses as Amber and Evan are looking at him questioningly in silence. He anticipates their next question and continues."You are making the air unbreathable -- just one of the problems -- the water, undrinkable. You are exhausting your resources necessary to sustain life, faster then any other civilization ever has and growing in population to unsustainable proportions." There is a long pause.

Amber, only too well, realizes where this is going. "With all these dreadful realities, what good is the energy source? It will not stop anything. It would only provide a platform to use more energy, would it not?"

"You are correct," Arturo replies. "According to my observations, it is almost too late for change, if not impossible."

"That is a disastrous statement and offers no hope for a future. I hope you are not talking about the end of all?"

There is indecipherable smile on Arturo's lips, a sign of combined sadness and despair. "Oh, definitely, not the end of all. The universe will continue to exist with some small evolutionary changes. The planet Earth? That is another question. A question I am not able to answer. I can only speculate on that."

"What can we do?" Amber asks quietly, without the usual spunk in her voice.

Arturo is very calm. His comforting voice does, however, continue to be one of caution. "Your democratic system is failing. In an attempt to be the big brother of freedom and democracy on this planet earth." Arturo leans forward. "You have failed in your own country. With all the political rhetoric and good-will, you have failed to stop the proliferation of all those things that bring civilizations to their knees."

"That's doomsday preaching, is it not?" Amber asks.

"Doomsday?" Arturo smiles sardonically. "There is no such word for the universe. It can apply to planets, however. When beings anywhere in this space of The All lose their connection to the creator, God the All, those specks of dust all around us ..." Arturo raises his hand and with a grand gesture sweeps the air pointing to the sky ... "they simply disappear."

"This is pretty heavy stuff, Arturo. Obviously, something we have to cope with. What about the energy source? What will happen? Will it help us?"

Arturo was prepared for this question. "Entirely up to your leaders and your scientists. If, within this next administration, appropriate changes have not taken place, the source will simply disappear. An easy task since, while the government has it in its possession, the Society, and that includes you, will always remain in control of it."

Amber and Evan look at each other, ready to ask some more questions but Arturo Smith is no longer there. He has simply vanished, or can Amber and Evan just not see him?

About the Author

"From Roswell With Love", is author Bill Rebane's first novel and departure from screenplay writing and his well rounded career in the motion picture industry. His roles as head of a major independent distribution organization, studio owner, producer, and director of 10 feature films, most of which he wrote. Many of these have become cult classics today. Born in Latvia of Estonian origin, he was educated in Germany. He came to the United States in 1952. His first book, a professional book "Film Funding 2000", became a valuable information tool for up and coming film makers and provided the impetus to expend his writing efforts to include the novelization of controversial and timely subject matters most interesting to him as a world travel and connoisseur of world affairs.

Made in the USA
Charleston, SC
03 November 2011